CHAPTER ONE

SALLY jumped with fright at the bang! What was *that*?

Her hands tightened on the steering-wheel of her Mercedes Benz as the car started to shake violently. She swerved in an effort to control the vehicle as she rapidly decreased speed. As she braked, the rear of her car fishtailed off on the wet, slick road. The rain was quite steady and her windscreen wipers were working overtime. Sally concentrated harder. She *had* to retain control, otherwise there might be a terrible accident!

Her heart was pounding wildly in her chest as her brain automatically sent out signals not to panic. The sound of squealing tyres behind her increased her tension. Thankfully she was in the left-hand lane. Sally managed to manoeuvre the car into the emergency stopping lane. The concrete barrier that marked the edge of the road loomed closer and Sally jerked the wheel around, hoping to avoid it, but to no avail.

Metal grated against concrete but finally Sally managed to bring the car safely to a halt. Her breathing was erratic as she just sat there in amazement. Her body started to tremble and she was positive her fingers had permanently fixed themselves around the steering-wheel.

She closed her eyes and allowed a little sob to bubble up and escape. Her lower lip began to tremble and she wondered, not for the first time, whether her move from Sydney to Canberra had been a good one.

When the door to the driver's side of her car was suddenly wrenched open, Sally screamed in fright. A man with dark hair that was slowly becoming wet from the heavy rain thrust his face close to hers.

'You're conscious. Good.'

Sally's adrenaline was still reeling from his unexpected appearance.

'*You scared me!*' she practically yelled at him.

'At least your senses are working well. A good sign.'

Sally's sluggish mind registered his words but her gaze was drawn to his eyes. They were blue. A deep, mesmerising blue. She looked at his lips and saw they were pressed firmly together. His nose was slightly crooked, indicating a break in the past, and his brow was creased into a thoughtful frown.

'I'm a doctor,' he informed her. 'Out you get.' His words were said softly but with an air of authority that brooked no argument.

Sally couldn't move. Her hands were still clenched around the steering wheel and her body was completely refusing to respond to the signals her brain was sending.

'Right,' the stranger said, as though summing up her situation. 'You're still too shocked to move.' With that, he leaned in further, unclasping her hands from the wheel. As his slightly wet hands covered her own, Sally felt a spark of desire shoot up her arm.

Sally could only stare up at him in amazement. Her breathing, which had just started to return to normal, began to increase once more but this time for a completely different reason.

He placed her hands in her lap before stretching his body across hers, his neck and face close to her own, and as Sally breathed in, the scent of his aftershave teased her senses.

Her eyelids fluttered closed as he released the clasp of her seat belt, his deep voice muttering, 'At least you were wearing your seat belt.'

Sally breathed in deeply again, savouring the scent, the warmth, the way his voice had washed over her like a warm blanket. Who *was* this man? She'd never experienced such an instant and overpowering reaction like this to *anyone*!

'Hey,' he called. 'Don't pass out on me now.' Two warm and sure fingers pressed themselves to the carotid pulse on Sally's neck. She opened her eyes and he smiled down at her.

The action softened the hard lines around his face and made the colour of his eyes more intense.

'Pulse is a bit fast but you'll live.' Their gazes locked for a whole five seconds that seemed to last for an eternity.

'Do you have an umbrella?' He broke the contact and, not waiting for her to answer, looked around the car. He spied the one she'd used earlier. Sally had shaken the water off before wrapping it in a plastic bag so the floor mat behind the front passenger seat didn't get wet. She'd been attempting to see some of Canberra's sights, but unfortunately the weather hadn't wanted to co-operate. Now it was starting to get dark.

'Stay there. I'll get it.'

Sally was slightly disappointed that he didn't slide his entire body across hers in order to reach the umbrella. Instead, he opened the rear door and leaned down to get it. Taking it out of the bag, he flicked it open.

'No sense in both of us getting wet.'

He held out his free hand to her and Sally tentatively accepted it. She was thankful that she'd dressed properly for this awful weather. Holding firmly onto his hand, trying hard to ignore the spiral of desire that once again ripped through her as they made physical contact, Sally swung one designer boot-clad foot out of the car.

She shifted around and placed her other foot onto the wet road. Her hand grasped firmly in his, she gingerly tested that her legs would support her before venturing to stand.

As she ducked her head to climb out of the car, Sally slowly stood, her gaze travelling along the hard, muscled lines of her knight in shining armour who was standing very close to the open door, umbrella overhead.

His denim jeans fitted him snugly, even more so considering they were very wet. His cotton shirt was completely drenched and had moulded itself to his finely sculptured torso. When she was out and standing beside him, he appraised her attire.

Sally knew her designer jeans, shirt and jumper, as well as the stylishly sleek boots, were an asset to her present predicament.

'At least you're dressed appropriately for this weather,' he remarked softly, once she was standing beside him. He released her hand and raked it through his now very wet hair. A few bits stood on end but it was short enough not to make him look ridiculous. Quite the contrary, Sally thought. He was, undoubtedly, the most devastatingly handsome man she had ever set eyes on...and in her thirty-four years she'd seen her fair share of good-looking men!

'Are you in any pain? Your neck?' he asked, his gaze watching her intently.

Sally was momentarily touched by his concern before she recalled he was a doctor. Still, he *was* making sure she felt all right.

'I'm fine. A little shaky but...fine.' Her words came out as a breathless whisper and she self-consciously cleared her throat. 'Fine,' she reiterated in a more normal tone. 'I don't know what happened. There was a loud bang and then suddenly I was swerving.'

'Your rear tyre blew out,' he stated, and then offered as an explanation, 'I was driving a few cars behind you when I noticed you starting to swerve. I pulled off the road in case medical assistance was required.'

'I'm glad you did,' she replied with a small smile.

'Do you have a phone?'

'Yes. Why?'

'Because you'll need to call a tow truck.'

'Oh. Is the damage *that* bad?' Sally asked as she knelt on the driver's seat and reached across for her handbag. Finding her phone, she looked around at the stranger, waiting for his reply. Instead, she was both surprised and somehow delighted to find his gaze intently watching her denim-clad *derrière*. She straightened and he quickly shifted his gaze.

'What did you say?' He frowned and then answered his own question. 'Damage. Yes, it's probably worse than you anticipate. Get whatever you need out of your car, lock it and we'll take a look.'

Sally bristled slightly at his tone. This man was obviously

used to giving orders *and* having them obeyed. After being raised by a domineering father, this was exactly the type of man she usually avoided.

He waited for her to do as he'd suggested before placing his free hand beneath her elbow and together, huddled beneath the umbrella, they walked around to survey the damage.

Dictatorial or not, Sally rationalised, his firm and perfect body so close to hers was having a devastating effect on her equilibrium.

As they rounded to the rear of the car, Sally gasped as she looked at the damage. The entire side of her green Mercedes was completely scratched.

'It could have been so much worse,' he pointed out.

'Yes, of course,' Sally responded quickly. 'But as you say, if I hadn't been able to get off the road and in this weather...' She let the sentence trail off and shuddered at the thought of what *might* have happened. She'd seen the results of horrific accidents far too many times.

'Look at that tyre,' he said, pointing and shaking his head in surprise at the burst rubber. 'You must have driven over something quite sharp for it to blow like that.' He looked out to the wet, black road that still had cars travelling over it. 'Whatever it is, it's probably still out there on the road.'

'Waiting to cause another accident. Glass perhaps?'

'Something like that. I hate to tell you this, but you're not going anywhere with a tyre like that. Call the tow truck and we'll wait in my car.'

Again his overbearing attitude riled her. Sally gritted her teeth. 'Thanks, but you don't have to wait.' She reached out to take the umbrella from him. 'I appreciate your help but I'm sure you have things you need to do this evening.'

The stranger frowned at her, retaining his hold on her umbrella. 'Are you dismissing me?'

'I just don't want to hold you up any longer,' she reasoned.

'It's OK.' He continued to clutch the umbrella tightly and Sally dropped her hand back to her side. 'I'll wait with you until the tow truck arrives so you're not left stranded.'

Sally realised that he was genuine. It surprised her. 'Thank you,' she said a little hesitantly. 'That's nice.'

'I have sisters,' he offered by way of explanation with a nonchalant shrug. 'Besides, my mother brought me up to always lend a helping hand.'

Sally found herself laughing. 'Then, please, thank your mother for me also.'

'Let's get to my car. It's better than standing out here, freezing and getting wet.'

She thought about it and realised he was right but her natural sense of caution held her back. This man, although helpful and nice, was still a stranger. However, she couldn't shake the feeling that they'd met before, which she knew was impossible because if they had she'd have *certainly* remembered.

A loud, blaring horn interrupted her thoughts and they both saw a flash of red skidding across the road in their direction.

'Look out!' the stranger called, and pushed Sally backwards. The red car crashed directly into the driver's side of Sally's car. A loud scream escaped from her lips as she realised that had she still been sitting in it, she would now be dead.

The Mercedes jerked at the contact and the tall, dark and handsome stranger was knocked to the ground. Sally rushed to his side and picked up the umbrella he'd dropped.

'You OK?'

'Yeah.' He stood.

The red car had now come to a stop after spinning into the concrete wall. The contact with the wall had smashed the rear end like a sardine can. The driver's side was jammed against the concrete wall, facing Sally's wrecked car. The horn in the red car was blaring.

'He's probably unconscious,' the stranger surmised. Leaving Sally with the umbrella, he sprinted across to the red car.

Sally's cold and wet fingers fumbled for her car keys. The collision of the red car with her Mercedes had triggered the alarm. She pressed the alarm switch to deactivate the annoying sound before sticking a key into the boot of her car—the only part, it seemed, that wasn't wrecked. Reaching for her well-stocked emergency medical kit, Sally followed the stranger.

'The driver's unconscious and trapped,' the man informed her. 'Call the ambulance and police.' Sally held the umbrella over him, even though he was well and truly drenched. 'I'm going to try and get in through the passenger window as the door's jammed.'

Sally took a heavy-duty torch from her medical kit and handed it to him. 'Use this to break the window.' She called triple zero and informed the operator of the situation.

When the window had been broken she took off her jumper, which had cost an absolute fortune, and placed it over the doorframe to protect them. 'I don't think you'll fit,' Sally said loudly to make sure she was heard over the blaring horn. 'I'll go.'

'What?' He looked at her as though she'd lost her marbles. 'Are you trained in accident procedures?' His voice radiated disbelief at her stupidity for even suggesting such a thing.

'I'm an orthopaedic surgeon,' she responded impatiently. 'Help me in.' Sally placed one leg through the window but required help to get her other leg through.

'Put your arm around my neck and I'll lift you,' he ordered. She did as he'd asked and when their heads were close to-gether—her arm around his neck as his arms encircled her waist—he grumbled into her ear, 'Your name wouldn't be Sally, would it?'

She turned her head and gazed at him, their mouths only millimetres apart.

'So we *do* know each other?' she said quietly with amaze-ment, before he deposited her into the car.

'Status?' he asked briskly, forcing her to keep her mind on the job at hand. He placed the medical kit inside the car, keep-ing it out of the rain, and poked his head through the window.

Sally turned to face the patient. 'Caucasian male. Early twenties,' she said, directing her words back to the stranger so she could be heard. She pressed two fingers to the patient's carotid pulse. 'Pulse fast but firm.' She eased his head back off the steering-wheel and the blaring sound of the horn stopped. 'Can you hear me?' she called, but received no response.

'Gash to upper right temple, will require sutures. Torch,' she requested, and stuck her hand out. In an instant she felt the cool, thin medical torch being placed firmly into her palm. She checked the young driver's pupils. 'Contracting to light.' She shone the light around the area. 'Legs aren't crushed, from what I can see. Right arm doesn't look too good, though. It's jammed between the door and the steering-wheel. Pass me the neck brace.'

She waited for him to do so before saying, 'So, as you obviously know who I am, would you mind telling me who you are?'

'You don't want to play twenty questions?' he asked as she secured the brace around the young man's neck.

'Not particularly.'

'Well, Dr Sally Bransford...' he said slowly, as though trying to draw things out. Sally felt a prickle of apprehension wash over her as she realised this man really *did* know who she was. She held her breath and waited for him to continue.

'As of tomorrow I'll be your new boss.'

Sally's jaw dropped open and she quickly closed it, looking over her shoulder at him with astonishment. 'Jed McElroy,' she whispered. 'No wonder you looked familiar. I can see the family resemblance quite clearly now. This gash on his head needs a bandage.'

Jed and Sally worked together, Jed handing her the things she needed while Sally fixed up their patient.

'What a way to meet,' she murmured. 'Jordanne will never believe it.'

'Oh she'll believe it, all right,' Jed replied. 'My sister appreciates irony in any form.'

'So...*boss*,' Sally asked once she'd finished applying the bandage. 'Do you want me to try and get to his arm?'

'I think I can hear sirens. Stay with him.'

Jed disappeared and Sally mumbled to herself, 'Where else do you expect me to go?'

This made everything different. Sally bent her head and closed her eyes. Unbelievable. The man who had stopped to help her was not only a man with a name but a name she knew! She lifted her head, fluffed her short blonde hair back into position and straightened her shoulders. Regardless of the feelings she'd experienced towards Jed when she'd first met him, they were to be pushed aside. The man would be her *boss* for the next twelve months!

One of her best friends was Jordanne McElroy, Jed's younger sister, and it was Jordanne who had set up the job between the two of them. Sally had moved to Canberra to complete her Ph.D. in sports medicine. Jed would not only be her supervisor but her boss as she'd be working alongside him in both his private and public practices.

Sally reached around for the medical kit which was now digging into her back. Shifting her position so she was sitting more comfortably in the squashed-in passenger seat, Sally pulled out her portable sphygmomanometer and stethoscope. She pumped up the cuff and slowly released it, watching the dial closely. Ninety over fifty. Not good.

The young man before her started to groan. 'Can you hear me?' Sally asked, and he groaned again. His eyelids opened momentarily and he stared hazily at Sally before closing them again.

'The ambulance has arrived and the police are blocking off the area,' Jed said.

'Good.'

'How's he doing?'

'BP ninety over fifty. He regained consciousness for a few moments but that was it. Now that the ambulance is here I'd like to set up an IV and give him some morphine.'

'OK. I'll organise that.'

'He may also need a blood transfusion. I can't see any blood but who knows what's happening around that arm?'

'Acknowledged. You'll need to stay with him until the last

possible moment. Chances are they'll need to take the top off the car to get him out.'

'Not a problem.'

Sally waited for Jed and the paramedics to organise the IV and morphine, knowing that they'd be checking and rechecking the doses. Finally, the saline IV was passed through the window and Sally began setting things up.

'Can you hear me?' she asked her patient for what seemed to be the hundredth time, and still didn't receive an answer. She'd checked everywhere, as was protocol, for a medical alert bracelet or other information regarding the patient's personal and medical details, but had found nothing. There was no wallet in his back pockets for identification and she'd found nothing in the glove box—not even car registration!

'Right. I'm going to be putting a needle into your left arm to set up a drip. This way we can administer analgesics which will hopefully diminish the pain you're feeling.' In this situation, whether the patient was conscious or not, Sally always informed them of what she was about to do.

She called to Jed and he leaned into the car to assist her in the procedure. Once the IV was in, Sally slowly administered the dose of morphine.

'There you go,' she said softly to her unconscious patient. 'That should help you to feel a bit better.'

Sally applied the BP cuff once more and pumped it up. The reading was the same. She checked his pupils and pulse as well. All still the same. One minute later, as the full effect of the morphine began to take effect, her observations told a different story.

'What's wrong?' Jed asked.

'BP is up.' She pressed her fingers to the patient's carotid pulse. 'Pulse rate is up. Narcan and oxygen stat. He's reacting to the morphine.'

The Narcan acted as an antidote to the morphine, and as Sally slowly administered it through the IV line Jed leaned his very wet torso into the car across Sally and managed to fit an oxygen mask around the patient's nose and mouth.

'Breathe deeply,' he commanded their unconscious patient. 'Come on, breathe deeply.'

As the Narcan slowly began to take effect, the patient's vital signs began to return to normal. Jed waited until Sally was free to take over the oxygen supervision before sliding back out of the car.

'I'll have the paramedics make a note immediately on his file that he's allergic to morphine.'

'Good. Is there a blanket out there? It's quite cool in here. I don't want him to get hypothermia as well.'

'I'll organise it.'

Jed was back within seconds, carrying blankets, and Sally draped them first around her patient as best she could, before placing one on herself. 'Police Rescue have arrived. They'll rig a tarpaulin over the roof so the patient won't get drenched when they take the top off.'

'Right.' Sally performed her neurological observations once more and was pleased with the results. She reported them to the paramedics who were taking notes of the situation and preparing for the removal of the patient. By the time they were ready to take the top off, Sally had decreased the oxygen but still left the mask over her patient's nose and mouth.

The noise as they took the roof off the car was awful, but Sally insisted on staying with her patient, blocking his ears. He roused momentarily just before they were ready to lift him but slipped back into oblivion once more.

The paramedics, along with the police rescue staff, lifted the patient out and manoeuvred him onto a stretcher. Sally's legs were aching from being cramped in the squashed car for so long.

'Agh,' she groaned after she'd been carried from the car. She was standing by the open back doors of the ambulance, a blanket wrapped around her shoulders, her umbrella over-head.

'What's the matter?' Jed asked, not looking up from his ministrations to their unknown patient. 'Have you hurt your-self anywhere?'

'No. Just pins and needles. How's his arm?'

'Fractured scapula, radius and ulna. I've stabilised the bleeding but his shoulder has been dislocated. X-rays are the next step so let's get him to hospital.'

Sally's teeth started chattering as the wind began to pick up, and she gathered the blanket tighter around her. She wasn't all that wet. The lower part of her jeans were the worst off.

'Cold, isn't it?' one of the paramedics said rhetorically, not looking at her as he focused on assisting Jed with the patient. 'That wind is coming straight off the snow-topped Brindabellas,' he continued. 'Make sure you stay as warm as possible.'

'He's ready for transfer,' Jed announced before Sally could reply to the paramedic. 'Sally and I will follow in my car so we'll see you boys at the hospital,' he said, and climbed out of the ambulance. He crossed to the policeman in charge and Sally followed him.

'So if we can leave the rest of this mess in your capable hands, we'll get going to the hospital.'

'Sure. What about this car?' The policeman asked, gesturing to the Mercedes.

Sally opened her mouth to speak but found her jaws almost frozen together. Her teeth chattered as she tried to talk but nothing happened.

'Here.' Jed took his wallet out of his back pocket and slid a white business card out. He handed it to the policeman. 'Here are my details. Dr Bransford starts work for me tomorrow.'

'Where do you want it towed to?' This time the policeman spoke directly to Jed, as though Sally were completely incompetent. It riled her but the fact of the matter was, she was so cold she *couldn't* talk.

'Take it to the Mercedes dealership in Fyshwick. They have a crash repair division.'

'Right you are, Doc. Thanks for your help.' This time the policeman's gaze included Sally as well, and she felt a little bit compensated.

'Let's get you somewhere warmer,' Jed said to Sally and led the way to his car. She hadn't noticed it until now, even though she'd subconsciously known it was there. It was a white Jaguar XJ6. He unlocked the door for Sally and, after prising the umbrella from her cold, wet fingers, he held it while she climbed in. The instant relief from the cool wind was warming. Huddling beneath the blanket, she felt herself begin to thaw.

She heard Jed open the boot and then close it again. A second or two later, the driver's door was flung open and some towels were hastily arranged on the seat before he sat down and closed the door.

Jed held a dark sports bag in his hands and Sally watched as he pulled out another dry towel and began to rub his hair dry.

Sally didn't know what to say, so she simply stared at him. He was so unlike any man she'd ever met. In the short time they'd spent together, Jed McElroy had managed to evoke quite a wide range of emotions within her.

He finished rubbing his hair and wiped the towel over his arms. His hair was standing more on end than before and Sally smiled to herself.

Jed looked up at her and she quickly hid the smile. 'I just want to change before I start to get too cold,' he explained. He pulled a thick, well-worn jumper out of the bag before unbuttoning his shirt. Each passing second, more of his hard chest was being revealed. Sally swallowed convulsively, her breathing becoming unsteady.

She choked, then coughed as his entire torso was revealed. He pulled the shirt from his arms and gave his bare skin another quick rub with the towel. Sally was transfixed. She'd never been around a man who simply stripped off in front of strangers.

His gaze flicked up to meet hers and Sally sharply turned her head to look out of the window. Due to the bleak day outside, the window acted as a mirror.

He pushed his arms into the jumper before lifting it over

his head and sliding it down his body, then stuffed everything back into the bag and threw it into the back seat. 'Let's get going,' he stated.

At the sound of his voice Sally turned to look at him, only to find him still looking at her. Blue eyes met blue eyes and for a split second neither of them moved. Sally felt the faint stirrings of the desire that had attacked her senses before. Jed McElroy was *dangerous*. Her mind processed this thought but she quickly pushed it away. Jed was nothing more than her best friend's brother as well as her new boss.

'I guess I'll be picking you up for work tomorrow morning,' he drawled, before starting the engine.

CHAPTER TWO

As JED'S Jaguar purred along the wet roads towards Canberra General Hospital, Sally tried not to feel uncomfortable at his last words. Jed would pick her up for work! She wondered exactly how long it would take to get her car fixed because at the moment she wanted it ready by eight a.m. tomorrow morning. Jed McElroy was someone she needed to keep at a professional distance, not someone who would be picking her up for work.

After everything that had happened in the past few hours, on top of the fact that she'd only just arrived in the Australian Capital Territory the previous evening, Sally was beginning to feel rather drained.

Jed turned on some soothing music, severing the need to make polite conversation. Sally rested her head back and closed her eyes. Although she was used to feeling fatigued due to long hours at the hospital, this was a new type of stress that her body had to deal with. She focused on breathing deeply, the car's heater warming her thoroughly.

'Sally?'

She heard the faint sounds of a very deep voice that she instantly recognised as Jed's. She smiled to herself and snuggled into the blanket, feeling more content than before. He certainly was a good-looking man, there was no doubt about that.

'Sally?' His voice was softer this time, more caring, and she loved the way her name sounded on his lips. It was said with sensuality…with vibrancy…with promise.

'Mmm,' she murmured, her smile increasing as she felt his warm hand touch her shoulder.

'Sally. Wake up.' He gave her a little shake. 'We're here. We're at the hospital.'

Sally jerked upright in her chair, the blanket slipping from around her. 'Huh?' She gazed blindly outside, into the darkness of the rain. It all came back with a rush. Her car was wrecked, they had a patient who required an operation and she was sitting not half a metre away from Jed McElroy—her new boss.

She turned to look at him as the haziness of her mind began to clear. He frowned at her and she had the distinct impression he wasn't too happy about something.

'We're at the hospital,' he repeated. 'Let's go check on the patient.' With that, he climbed from the car and shut the door behind him. Sally pushed the blanket from her legs and quickly scrambled from the car into the rain. He'd parked behind the ambulance in the emergency bay, and as they entered the hospital's accident and emergency department she saw him give a cheery wave to an orderly, before tossing his keys in the same direction.

Jed walked into the examination cubicle, Sally not too far behind him.

'Sorry, lady,' a young man said to her. He had long blond hair, pulled back into a ponytail, and wide green eyes. His white coat and hospital badge told Sally his name was Peter Jacobs and that he was an intern. 'Family need to wait out in the waiting room.'

Sally looked at Jed but he was deep in discussion about the patient's arm with another tall, dark and handsome stranger.

'I'm not family—' she began, but he cut her off.

'I don't care who you are, this area is for hospital staff only.'

His tone was one that Sally didn't much care for. Even if she *had* been part of their unknown patient's family, Dr Jacobs shouldn't be talking to her in this manner.

Sally straightened her shoulders and levelled him with a glare, which could have been quite difficult since he was at least four inches taller than her own five-feet-seven build, but she was used to dealing with people like him, regardless of how tall and intimidating they first appeared.

'As I was saying,' she said crisply and clearly, 'before you *rudely* interrupted me, I'm not a member of this patient's family or an acquaintance of any other sort.' Her tone and stature made the young intern's attitude change. 'My name is *Dr* Sally Bransford—or rather *Mr*, if you prefer, considering I'm a qualified orthopaedic surgeon.'

The intern's pallor grew white and he swallowed nervously.

'Personally,' Jed said as he crossed to her side, the still unconscious patient being wheeled off to Radiology, 'I think you should stick with ''Doctor'', rather than ''Mister'', Sally. You're much too...' he paused thoughtfully, his gaze radiating mischief '...decidedly feminine for the title of ''Mister''!'

There was a loud rumble of mirth from the man standing directly behind Jed. 'Hear! hear!' He placed a hand on Jed's shoulder. 'I'd suggest you have your teabreak now, Dr Jacobs,' the other man ordered. 'We'll be in Theatre once our unknown patient gets back from Radiology.'

As the intern scuttled away, the man asked, 'Well, Jed, aren't you going to introduce us?' He eyed Sally with curiosity, although there was nothing remotely sensual in his gaze.

'Alex Page, meet Sally Bransford, my new Ph.D. student and right-hand...er...man for the next twelve months.'

Sally was surprised at Jed's teasing manner. Perhaps around his friends, he was more easygoing—more relaxed.

Alex shook Sally's hand. 'I'm very pleased to meet you. I'm the clinical director of the orthopaedic department here at the hospital,' Alex continued, 'so I guess we'll be seeing each other around.'

Sally liked him instantly and hoped they would become friends. Good-looking he certainly was, but in her opinion he didn't set off any bells and whistles—unlike Jed.

'Alex is still tossing around the idea of hiring a research fellow for twelve months.'

'Jed suggested it and I've been investigating funding. So if it doesn't work out with Jed, you could always come and work here with me.'

'Stop it,' Jed growled, and Sally was surprised at the fierceness of his tone. He cleared his throat and forced a smile. 'Stop trying to steal my staff,' he warned Alex.

'Why wouldn't it work out with Jed?' she asked, a small smile on her lips.

'He's just trying to steal you so he doesn't have to go through the rigmarole and red tape of finding a lackey of his own.'

'So I'm to be your lackey, am I?' Sally asked, thoroughly enjoying this teasing side to Jed.

He looked at her for a moment and his gaze flashed briefly with heated desire before it was quickly veiled. 'Basically.' He nodded.

'Glad we got that cleared up now. So, *my lord and master…*'

Alex laughed at her words.

'What's the verdict on the patient?'

'Alex is on call and will take over his treatment.'

Sally watched Jed carefully. Was he turning the patient's treatment over to Alex because he knew she was exhausted? Did he really *care* about that? During internship, she would have worked eighty-hour weeks so it wasn't that she couldn't handle her fatigue. Then again, she rationalised, forcing herself to stop being overly sensitive, it would be hospital protocol to hand over to the surgeon on call—who just happened to be Alex.

'So we're off the hook?' She directed her question to Alex, who nodded.

'Go home and get some sleep. You're going to need all your wits about you tomorrow.' He added in a stage whisper, 'I hear your boss is a tyrant.'

Sally couldn't help herself and laughed at his words. 'Good advice. I'll just call a taxi.' She looked at Jed. 'I've already burdened you enough.'

'Don't be silly,' he said, frowning. 'My car is right outside and I'll need to know where you live so I can pick you up in the morning.'

'Really, Jed. Taxis will be fine until my car is fixed.' Sally was conscious of Alex watching their conversation with increasing delight.

'You'd better let him take you home, Sally. Jed has a strong protective instinct installed deep within him. I guess it comes from being the eldest of five siblings—but, then, you'd know that.'

So Alex knew about her relationship with Jordanne. Interesting!

'Fine,' she acquiesced. Holding out her hand to Alex, she said, 'It was nice to meet you.'

'You, too. Say, if you're not busy this coming Saturday, how about dinner?'

Sally opened her mouth to respond but Jed interrupted.

'She'll be busy.'

'Excuse me?' Sally frowned, stunned at his audacity. 'So, because I'm your *lackey*, this means you control *all* of my time?'

'No. I'm on call on Saturday.'

'And you need Sally to hold your hand while you operate?' Alex teased. Sally didn't miss the dagger look that Jed shot his friend. 'Perhaps we can arrange some other time,' Alex said to Sally, a wide grin on his face.

'Sounds good,' she responded, now determined to go out with Alex purely to annoy Jed.

'We're leaving,' Jed announced, catching Sally's elbow in his hand which forced her to walk with him.

Sally waved goodbye to Alex and shrugged out of Jed's grasp. She was fuming at his high-handedness. Jordanne had often told her that Jed was over-protective but she had news for Jed McElroy—*she* was *not* one of his sisters!

She waited until they were seated in the car, driving out of the hospital's gates, before turning slightly in her chair to face him.

'Where to?'

'Carella Court in Manuka,' she said in a clipped tone. 'Do you know it?' He simply nodded. Sally waited a moment, and when he didn't say anything else she asked, 'Do I expect an apology from you?'

'For what?'

'Just as I thought,' she said quietly to herself.

'Pardon?'

'You don't see that you've done anything wrong, do you?'

'I have no idea what you're talking about, Sally.'

'Then let me spell it out for you,' she replied, trying to keep a tight rein on her temper. 'I am *not* one of your sisters.'

'I know.'

'Then why are you playing the protective big brother? Who I decide to date is really none of your business.'

'When it interferes with your work, it most definitely *is* my business.'

'What? How can going out on a date with Alex possibly be interfering with my work—work, I might add, that I haven't even begun yet.'

'It's not a date, Sally.'

'Pardon?' She frowned at him.

'Alex has a policy where he takes new surgical staff members out for dinner when they first start working at Canberra General.' Jed's tone was bland, as though he was bored with the entire conversation.

Sally was silent for a moment, digesting this information. 'Well, if it's a common occurrence, why were you so…defensive?'

'Defensive? I wasn't being defensive,' he denied with a shrug of his shoulders. He stopped at a red light. 'Look, Sally, I know what type of background you come from so don't give me your high-and-mighty attitude.'

Sally gasped at his words, amazed at what she was hearing.

'With regard to Alex,' he went on, 'make another time to have your business dinner. I'm on call on Saturday night at the hospital, and as this will be your first week here you should be at the hospital with me to see how things are handled.'

'I don't start in your employ until tomorrow,' Sally countered, choosing to ignore his blatant dig at her background. 'What right do you have to say what I can do and when?'

'I'm your employer,' he reasoned, but when the light turned green, he planted his foot down hard on the accelerator. Sally gripped the seat as they took off, but to her surprise Jed remained right on the speed limit.

Both of them were silent for a while before Jed cleared his throat and spoke.

'I apologise if I came on a bit strong. As you don't know what your schedule is and I do, I didn't think twice about mentioning you wouldn't be available on Saturday night. Otherwise you would have made plans with Alex and then had to change them.'

'Something I'm more than capable of doing myself,' she pointed out.

'All right. I promise never to interfere in your private life again. *Satisfied?*' Jed took the corner a little too fast and the tyres squealed in protest.

Was that what she wanted? Sally knew she was desperately attracted to Jed but that didn't mean she wanted him telling her what she could and couldn't do. Having grown up with a domineering father, who had *always* told her exactly what to do, Sally had rebelled against anyone else treating her in this fashion.

He pulled the Jaguar into the driveway of Carella Court. 'What number is your town house?'

The court was beautifully landscaped with lush green gardens. Sally had been told the gardens had won design awards and been featured on the cover of several gardening magazines. She couldn't wait until spring, when the flowers would be in full bloom.

'Number four.' Sally gestured to the building second on the right. Jed brought the car to a stop outside and cut the engine.

Sally released her seat belt and rummaged in her bag for her keys. She turned to look at Jed, a polite 'thank you' on her lips, but when her gaze met his, something else hap-

pened—she was again struck by how undeniably handsome he
was.

He was still sitting in profile to her and Sally's heartbeat
increased as she looked once more at the classic lines of his
face. Butterflies appeared to be living in her stomach and they
took flight the instant his gaze met her own.

Sally's mouth became suddenly dry and she slipped her
tongue between her lips to wet them. 'Um,' she breathed with
uncertainty, and then tried to pull herself together. This was
the man she would be working alongside for the next twelve
months—a man she wasn't even sure she *liked*—but of one
thing Sally was certain. Her attraction to Jed was real and it
was going to be difficult to fight.

With her hand fumbling for the doorhandle, Sally cleared
her throat and mumbled, 'Goodbye.' Then she opened the door
and climbed out of the car. She shut the door smoothly and,
without a backward glance, hurried to her front door. Fitting
the key into the lock, she was inside and pressing her back
against the hard, wooden door within an instant.

A moment or two later, the Jaguar purred quietly away and
out of the court. Sally remained where she was, allowing her
heart rate to return to normal. Something had to be done.
Something just *had* to be done.

Dropping her bag and keys onto the table, she quickly
crossed to her phone. Tapping in Jordanne's number, she waiting impatiently for her friend to pick up.

'Pick up, pick up,' she whispered through clenched teeth as
she began to pace the room, glad the phone was a cordless
one. She flicked on the heating, standing near the vent to warm
herself while Jordanne's phone rang on.

'Hello,' Jordanne's voice finally said.

'What took you so long?' Sally blustered into the receiver.

'Sorry, I was in the shower. Listen, can I call you back in
a few minutes? I just want to get dressed.'

'I guess so but hurry up,' Sally said impatiently.

'Sally? What's wrong?'

'Oh, nothing, really.' Sally took a breath and tried to calm herself. 'Get dressed and I'll call you back in a few minutes.'

'OK.'

Sally hung up and decided that as Jordanne was getting dressed, she might as well get changed into warmer and, more importantly, drier clothes than the ones she had on now. Switching on the kettle as she walked through to her room, Sally quickly changed into a warm fleecy tracksuit then made herself a soothing cup of herbal tea.

Getting comfortable, she pressed the redial button and was connected with Jordanne instantly.

'Right. What's happened?' Jordanne asked, not bothering with the pleasantries of 'hello'.

'I've had a terrible day,' Sally almost sobbed into the phone. 'My car is wrecked, I've had to assist with an accident and to top it all off…I met your brother.' Sally wailed the last part.

'Whoa!' Jordanne said with incredulity. 'Slow down and start from the beginning.'

Sally told Jordanne about the car accident and the ensuing havoc it had created. She told her friend about the arguments she'd already had with Jed and how he'd become protective when Alex had asked her out.

'They've been friends for years,' Jordanne explained, and Sally nodded.

'I thought as much. I don't fancy Alex or anything but it would be nice to make some new friends. You know how hard it is for me.'

'Yes, I do. Coming from a wealthy background, it hasn't been easy for the poor little rich girl, has it? It took me a while, though, to understand your way of thinking. I mean our backgrounds are so different. You're an only child and me…well, I've got too many siblings to count.' Jordanne laughed.

'Making new friends has never been easy for me.' Sally sighed. 'If you hadn't cut through my defences back in med school, I don't know what I would have done.'

'It wasn't easy. You were so smart but so aloof from everyone around you. I couldn't resist the challenge of making friends with you.'

Sally could tell Jordanne was smiling as they both remembered. 'You've always been a go-getter, Jordanne. I still can't believe that my father nearly ruined everything.'

'I wouldn't have *let* him ruin it.'

'I was horrified when I came downstairs from my room and found you talking to my father.' Sally shuddered at the memory—a memory that was over ten years old. Jordanne had come over to Sally's house on impulse to see if they could study together. The maid had shown Jordanne into the sitting room before going to fetch Sally. Unfortunately, Sally's father had just returned from a recent overseas trip and had come upon Jordanne waiting patiently for her friend.

'There's no way in the world your father would *ever* have been able to buy my co-operation. It was clear that you loved medicine and I wasn't going to be used as a pawn to persuade you to quit.'

'You were a good friend then and you're *still* a good friend,' Sally said.

'I guess that's when I began to understand your reticence to make new friends.'

'It was also the reason I never accepted the invitations to stay at your house. As much as I wanted to…' Sally shook her head emphatically '…I couldn't do it to your family. Not with my father's reputation for buying people off left, right and centre.'

'I know,' Jordanne sympathised. 'Now look at you. After ten years of a strong and solid friendship, you're working with my oldest brother. Oh, speaking of friendships,' Jordanne continued, 'have you spoken to Kirsten?'

'I tried calling her earlier today but she wasn't home, which is why I decided to go sightseeing. Terrible day. Rotten weather.' Sally childishly poked her tongue out at the curtain-covered window to the rain outside. 'I could have used an ally today. I'll try calling her again when I've finished talking to you. At least she lives in the same city as me. When are *you* going to take the plunge and move from Sydney?'

'Who knows?' Jordanne replied rhetorically. 'My job finishes soon and I don't have anything concrete as yet. Hey, while I remember, give me your new phone number.'

The two friends talked for a while longer and Sally began to feel better about the day. Jordanne was the one who had taught her to look for the silver lining in everything—even when things seemed awful. *This* was Sally's silver lining. Her friendship with Jordanne and Kirsten was as strong today as it had been back in med school.

Being the poor little rich girl, as Jordanne had often called her, had been no bed of roses. Many people had only been interested in Sally for her money and 'position in society'.

Sally made herself another cup of tea as she talked with Jordanne about anything and everything. She'd told her friend everything about her day—everything except one important little detail which she was determined to leave out. That being her undeniable attraction to Jed.

Jed threw his keys onto the table beside the door and stalked over to the phone. He tapped in his sister's number and growled when he received the engaged signal. He wondered, just for a moment, whether she was talking to Sally. It wouldn't surprise him. The two had been friends for years.

Deciding he'd try her later, he went into the bathroom, stripped off and stood under the hot spray of the shower. Slowly he began to thaw out and warm up. He closed his eyes and washed his hair. Visions of Sally Bransford entered his mind. Her blonde hair blowing in the breeze, her icy blue eyes melting as their gazes met and the way her body had fitted so perfectly next to his when he'd picked her up to help her into the wrecked car.

She was stunning, there was no denying it, but she was far too rich for his blood. The haughty attitude, the dismissiveness of her tone—he'd seen it all before. He should probably refuse to work with her—tear up the contract before she began work tomorrow morning. Why had he let Jordanne talk him into doing this? His little sister had been the one to suggest he take on the role of Sally's Ph.D. supervisor. Jed had declined at first, knowing of Sally's wealthy background, but his little sister had always been very persuasive—just like their mother—and Jed had been hard-pressed to say no to her. She'd pointed out the various benefits of having Sally around for the year, the main one being to lighten Jed's own work-load.

As a student under his direction, Sally would not only assist him in his private practice but at Canberra General Hospital as well. To top it all off, she would be focusing on her Ph.D. and conducting her research at the Institute of Australasian Sport where Jed was the leading orthopaedic surgeon to the athletes training for world and Olympic competitions.

Jed had read Sally's academic transcripts and been suitably impressed, but how many of her qualifications were real and not 'purchased' by her father? In the social circles he'd been forced to move in from time to time, he'd seen a few examples of the rich at work. When their children hadn't made the grade, the wealthy parent had simply made a sizeable donation to some hospital fund and, *voilà*, an instant pass for their children.

That was another reason he'd agreed to Jordanne's proposal. He wanted to see if Sally really did have the brains to carry out the research on her Ph.D. now that she was living further away from her powerful father.

Her thesis was to be on 'Upper Limb Injuries Resulting from Gymnastic Activity' and Jed had been intrigued with her outline for the study. Even if for nothing but the research, he'd decided to accept Sally as a student under his supervision.

Jed switched off the water and began to towel himself dry. Never had he expected her to be so unbelievably beautiful. When he'd first opened her car door after she'd swerved off the road, he'd felt as though he'd been struck by lightning. *Then*, considering he knew every orthopaedic surgeon who worked in Canberra, he'd instinctively known that this beautiful woman in his arms had been none other than his new student and right-hand man.

Jed dressed in dry clothes and made himself something to eat. The phone rang and he crossed to it, chewing his mouthful as he went. 'Dr McElroy.'

'Jed, it's Alex.'

'How's the patient?'

'We're just about to go into Theatre but everything looks routine. I just wanted to apologise for treading on toes when I asked Sally out for dinner.'

'Why apologise?' Jed's tone was terse. 'It's only a business dinner—a fact, I might add, which you forgot to mention to Sally. She thought you were asking her out on a date.'

'Well, you've obviously remedied that fact.'

'Yes. She now knows it's a business dinner and that you do it for everyone.'

'So why were you so vehement when I mentioned Saturday night?'

'I was *not* vehement,' he clarified forcefully, and raked his free hand through his hair. 'What is it with everyone tonight?' he mumbled.

'What was that?' Alex asked with particular interest.

'Nothing.'

'If you say so,' Alex acquiesced. 'The other reason I called was to make sure it was OK with you if I ask Sally out for a real date. You know, not just a business dinner.'

'Why wouldn't it be?' Jed answered, trying to keep his tone impersonal. The mental image of Sally sitting across a candlelit table from Alex, in a secluded corner of one of Canberra's finest restaurants, made his gut twist uncomfortably, and he immediately dismissed it.

'I was just wanted to check—you know, in case you fancy her yourself.'

'Are you having a go at me?' Jed demanded.

'Why would I be doing that?' Alex asked, feigning innocence.

'Wouldn't be the first time,' Jed muttered. 'Sally Bransford is yours for the taking, if you like that kind of thing.'

'What's not to like? She's an absolute stunner with that blonde hair and blue eyes a man could just lose himself in. She's intellig—'

'I didn't think blondes were your type,' Jed interrupted as he paced up and down.

'Ordinarily, they're not. They're more your type, I know. Brunettes are definitely more my flavour but there's just something about Sally...' He trailed off.

'Her money?' Jed suggested, and was immediately cross with himself for saying it. 'Forget that,' he added quickly.

'I should think so. How dare you imply that—?'

'I said forget it,' Jed replied with more force.

'Is anything wrong?'

Jed closed his eyes and shook his head in disgust at himself. When he didn't answer, Alex continued, 'Jed? You're a bit snappy today.'

'Leave it out, Page. The last thing I need right now is your amateur psychiatric analysis. Ask her out. I don't care.'

'Great. That's everything I wanted to know,' Alex replied sweetly, and disconnected the call.

Jed sat down and covered his hands with his eyes. Ever since he'd met her, he hadn't been able to get Sally off his mind. His stomach growled and he remembered his half-eaten dinner. Going to the kitchen, he found it stone cold. Reheating it in the microwave, he ate before trying Jordanne's number again. Thankfully she'd decided to get off the phone as it was now ringing.

'Hello?'

Keep it light, he told himself. 'Howdy, sis.' Jed knew that had Jordanne answered the phone when he'd first tried to call, they would have had a completely different conversation to the one they were about to have.

'Jed. Hey, big brother, how are you?'

'Fine. A little bit wet but fine nonetheless.'

'Raining again?' she asked.

'Yes.'

Jed was waiting for her to say something about Sally but Jordanne remained quiet. Perhaps she *hadn't* been talking to his new colleague.

'Busy day?' he asked.

'Sort of. I've been cleaning out my cupboards. Mum's organising a trash and treasure market for the church next Saturday so I wanted to give her some things to take.'

'Always giving, she is.'

'She's the best mum.'

Again there was silence. Not an uncomfortable one, but the longer it stretched, the more Jed couldn't broach the subject of Sally.

'Oh, just spit it out, Jed,' Jordanne said playfully. 'You've obviously called to discuss something with me. So—out with it.'

'You know me too well.' He laughed. 'Actually, there was something I wanted to discuss with you. How would you like to move to Canberra for twelve months?'

'Really? Why?'

'My friend, Alex, is looking for a research fellow for twelve months.'

'Interesting. Tell me more.'

'Well, I thought you'd be perfect for the job. You're a qualified orthopaedic surgeon and your contract with the hospital expires next month which is when this job will start. Also, it would look good on your résumé.'

'So what made you think of me?'

'Well, Alex jokingly offered the position to Sally which, of course, she couldn't take anyway because she's working with me for the next twelve months, and that's when I thought of you. After all, you were…' he paused to choose the right word '…beneficial in finding someone to help lighten my own workload. It's the least I can do for both you and Alex.'

'So does this mean you're happier about working with Sally? The last time we spoke you still had reservations.'

'I…feel…happier, yes,' he said slowly.

'Is that because you've met her?'

'So you *were* talking to her before. I knew it!'

'We're friends, Jed. What do you expect? Friends talk.' Jordanne chuckled. 'Quite a way to meet, if you ask me. I couldn't have planned it better, even if I'd tried.'

'We thought you'd like it.'

'So you don't find her snobby and too rich for your liking?'

'Quite the contrary. That's exactly how I find her.'

'Really?' Jordanne's tone radiated amazement. 'But Sally's so down-to-earth and she hasn't had an easy time of things in the past.'

'Oh, spare me the sob story. She's probably been given everything she's ever wanted and, as I've said before, baby-sitting a spoilt brat for twelve months isn't really my idea of fun.' He growled the words into the receiver, hoping that his sister wouldn't pick up on the fact that Sally Bransford was undoubtedly the most beautiful woman he'd ever met. She was also the most exasperating.

'Jed—she's not Anya,' Jordanne pointed out softly. 'Don't tar every rich woman you meet with the same brush.'

Jed ignored his sister's comments. 'Did she tell you I gave her a lift home? Did she?' He didn't wait for Jordanne to answer but continued, 'Not even a thank you. Just a haughty and dismissive "goodbye" before she all but sprints from the car.'

'Wasn't it raining?'

'All I wanted was a thank you. It's no big deal. You know how strict our parents have always been on manners. They cost nothing—'

'But mean so much,' Jordanne interrupted, finishing the sentence for him. 'Yes, I know, and it surprises me that Sally *didn't* say thank you. She's one of the most polite people I know—too polite sometimes, and that's when she comes across as snobby. Listen, Jed. Just give her a break. She's just moved to a new town, her car's been wrecked—'

'I know, Jordanne.' It was his turn to interrupt. 'I was *there*, remember.'

'Yes, yes, I do. Just be nice, all right? I really want this year to work out for both of you. Sally needs a good supervisor and someone who works closely with athletes so she can complete her thesis. You, on the other hand, need someone to help lighten your load. It's a win-win situation.' Jordanne stopped talking for a moment. 'My date's arrived. I'd better go.'

'Who is it? Do I know the guy?' Jed's instant protectiveness came to the fore.

'Jed,' Jordanne warned, and he knew to back off. She'd told him enough times—her private life was *her* private life! 'Get me some more information on that job with Alex—oh, and, *please*, make an effort to be nice to Sally. For me?'

'I'll try,' he responded. 'But that's all I'm going to do.'

'It's all I can ask. Bye. Love you.'

'Love you, too. Take care and have a fun date.' Jed hung up but sat on the couch for a while longer, thinking about his conversation with Jordanne and the time he'd spent with Sally.

Of one thing he was certain. If he wasn't careful around Sally Bransford, she'd end up using her beauty and charm to weave a spell around him—just as Anya had done almost ten years ago.

CHAPTER THREE

JED once more pressed his cold finger firmly onto the doorbell, holding it there for an extra second before releasing it. He'd left his thick, warm coat in the car as he hadn't anticipated standing out in the cold winter wind for any length of time. If Sally didn't hurry up and answer, he'd go without her. Perhaps, he thought as he rubbed his hands together, trying to keep them warm, she'd already left—taken a taxi like she'd said she would. Jed edged his ear closer to the door, listening for any signs of life.

The door was suddenly wrenched open and Jed jerked up-right. He met Sally's gaze and smiled politely. She'd caught him so off guard he'd forgotten his previous annoyance with her.

'Sorry,' she apologised. 'Jordanne just called to wish me luck for my first day at work.' She gestured to the phone she was still holding in her hand. 'I'll get my bag and then we can go.'

As she turned to do her tasks, Jed's gaze quickly travelled over the perfect curves of her body. He instinctively knew her navy suit had been tailor-made to fit, and the tailor had done an *excellent* job. Her short blonde hair was neat and tidy—perfect, just like everything else about the woman.

'Ready,' she announced as she walked towards him, her coat draped over her arm, her shoes not too high in the heel. 'Sensible' was the word he would have used to describe them, and he was glad she appeared to have *some* sense in that head of hers.

She flicked the bolt on the door and belatedly Jed realised she was waiting for him to move out of the way. He took a step back, calling himself all sorts of names for being drawn beneath her spell.

She took two steps towards the car before stopping.

'Oops. I forgot to set the alarm.' Sally rummaged around in her bag and pulled out a small remote control. She pressed a button and the alarm beeped, signalling it was on.

'I *must* get into the habit,' she mused out loud. 'Ready.' Sally smiled up at Jed, only to realise he was frowning at her. 'Something wrong?'

'No. No,' he repeated, and quickly walked to his car. Opening the door, he held it for her.

'Thank you,' she replied, now concerned that something was indeed wrong. Sally did her seat belt up and watched as Jed walked around to the driver's door. He looked every inch the tall, dark and handsome man that he was, especially in his charcoal grey suit. A gust of wind whipped his hair out of place and she longed to run her fingers through it, smoothing it back into place.

As Jed opened the door, sat down and did up his seat belt, Sally instinctively knew the strained atmosphere they'd experienced yesterday evening would be repeated. Jed McElroy obviously had a bee in his bonnet, and if that was the way he chose to behave, it was fine with her.

'Horrible weather,' she commented once he'd navigated the car onto the main road.

'It's July.' He didn't turn his head to look at her and Sally realised she was in for an...eventful day.

'How far is the clinic?'

'Ten minutes from here.'

'That's good,' she said with honest surprise. 'In Sydney, I used to travel at least forty to forty-five minutes one way.'

'This isn't Sydney.'

Sally counted to twenty in an effort to control her rising temper. The silence reigned as he continued to concentrate on his driving. What was wrong with him? She had just been trying to make idle conversation. There was nothing else for her to do except confront him.

'Jed?'

'Yes.' His answer was clipped.

'Is there something wrong?'

He didn't respond with words, he simply glanced at her.

'Is it something *I've* done? Because if I've inadvertently done something wrong, please, tell me.'

'As a matter of fact,' he said as he turned off the main road and headed down another, 'I was rather…annoyed when you didn't thank me for the ride home yesterday evening.'

'I didn't?' Sally was completely surprised at his words.

'No.' He stopped at a red light and turned slightly to face her. 'In my family, manners have always been of the utmost importance. I expect it from my family, my friends *and* my business colleagues. A simple please or thank you can go a long way. They cost nothing but mean so much. If we're going to work together successfully throughout this year, then manners are the one thing I will expect from you—otherwise you may as well go back home to Sydney.'

Sally was stupefied at his speech. She gaped at him, her mouth opening in amazement. He turned from her as the light changed to green.

'I…I apologise,' she murmured a few minutes later, still stunned at his words. 'I, too, am a firm believer in good manners. I can't think what came over me.' The instant the words were out of her mouth, Sally knew they were a lie. She knew exactly what had come over her last night when she'd turned to thank him for the ride. Therefore, it was really all *his* fault. If he wasn't so good-looking, so handsome, so sexy, she wouldn't have responded to him the way she had, which had in turn caused her to forget her manners.

'So…' She cleared her throat. 'Thank you, Jed, for the lift home last night and for driving me to work this morning. Jordanne told me you live quite close to your consulting rooms so I know it's out of your way to come and collect me. As I said yesterday, I don't expect it—'

'That's not the point,' he interrupted.

'I know, and although I might feel some guilt at you driving to Manuka simply to pick me up, I *do* appreciate it.'

He was silent until he'd parked the car in the underground car park beneath his sleek and stylish private practice. The building was quite large for a single orthopaedic practice but Sally remembered Jordanne telling her that two physiotherapists also worked in this practice with him.

'Apology accepted,' he said as he cut the engine and took the keys out. He opened the door without looking at her and climbed out of the car. Now it was Sally's turn to feel irked. The least he could have done was look at her when he'd spoken. He collected something from the boot. He turned and looked at her as she sat in the car, trying to control her anger once more.

Undoing her seat belt, she gathered her bag and coat before reaching for the doorhandle. A small gust of wind made her look around to find Jed standing there, holding her door open for her.

'Please, allow me to play chauffeur.' His tone held a hint of irritation as she alighted from the car.

'Thank you,' she replied clearly, in reference to their previous conversation.

'You're so welcome,' came his retort as he slammed the door, locked the car and set the alarm with the flick of a button, before striding off in the direction of a door.

'What have I done now?' Sally mumbled to herself as she followed him. The door led to a stairwell where they climbed a single flight of stairs and walked down a corridor, before entering the main lobby of the practice.

'The physios' rooms are to the left, my…er…our consulting rooms are to the right,' he explained as he continued to walk through the building. 'This will be your consulting room,' he said, opening a door and waiting for her to enter. The decor was tasteful and relaxing. There was a sink and cupboards, which were no doubt filled with all the supplies she'd need, as well as the examination couch and her desk for writing up notes. There was a computer and printer on the desk and she realised that, as many practices were doing nowadays, this one was completely computerised.

He must have been watching her gaze intently because he said, 'I hope there won't be a problem with the computer system. You did state on your résumé that you were familiar with the computer program we run here.'

'Yes, yes, I am,' she confirmed. 'It's great, Jed.'

He frowned at her praise. 'My room is down the corridor, the tearoom is in the middle. Toilets are out near the reception area.' He turned and disappeared from her sight. Sally walked over to her desk and opened the drawers, taking a look at what was inside. Pens, pencils, slips of paper, prescription pads, letterheads—all the stationery she'd require.

Sally quickly hung her coat up on the hook by the door before checking the waiting-room area. It was too early for patients. She went around the receptionist's desk and checked the diary, looking at her patient list for the day.

'It's going to be a busy day,' a female voice said from behind her.

Sally jumped and looked around.

'Sorry,' a thin lady with grey hair and sparkling brown eyes said. 'Didn't mean to scare you. I'm Vera Preston—Jed's receptionist. You must be Sally.'

Vera held out her hand to Sally who instantly smiled back and shook the proffered hand.

'Pleased to meet you.'

'As I said,' Vera continued as she placed her bag on the desk and took off her coat, 'you've got a busy day ahead. There are three new patients coming to the clinic this morning and you've got them all. The consultations for them will be longer than the rest. Has Jed explained any of this to you?'

'No. He's just shown me around.'

'He was going to explain the practice set-up as soon as he'd taken his coat off and switched the urn on,' Jed's deep voice said from behind both of them. 'Let's get a cuppa before it's time to start work.'

'I'll be there in a minute,' Vera said. 'I think I've already had one too many cups of coffee this morning.' She smiled at Sally before heading towards the toilets.

Sally and Jed went into the kitchen which had an urn, a coffee-machine and a sandwich toaster. There was also a two-ring gas stove and a large fridge.

'A well-equipped room,' Sally commented.

Jed shrugged. 'I like to cook. Sometimes when I'm working late I'll make myself a healthy meal.'

'Really?' Again, he'd surprised her.

'Let me guess,' he said, one eyebrow raised in mock amusement. 'You hate to cook and eat out at every available opportunity.'

'Yes.' Sally frowned. Had Jordanne told him *more* about her than she'd anticipated? The look he was giving her—that sardonic smile of his—was becoming more familiar, as was the weakening of her knees whenever he looked at her that way. 'How did you know?'

'Hmm. Figures.'

'What's that supposed to mean?' Sally felt her temper ignite at his audacity, the weakening of her knees disappearing in annoyance. Her frown intensified.

'Nothing.'

Vera chose that moment to join them so Sally was prevented from questioning him further. *What* figured?

After making them both a cup of tea, Vera continued to outline Sally's day. 'Also, there's a gymnast by the name of Alice Partridge who has a complaint so, considering your thesis studies, I've booked her in to see you.'

'Great.' Sally pushed aside her reaction to Jed, focusing on what Vera had said. A spark of excited enthusiasm started to bubble up.

'If you're unsure of anything, just ask,' Vera concluded as she checked her watch. 'I'll go and unlock the front door. Mrs Greeves is due in early to see you about that hip of hers,' she told Jed.

'That means my mother will be calling later today. Mrs

Greeves is one of her old schoolfriends,' he told Sally as Vera left them alone.

'Treating friends of your parents isn't common for you?'

'I don't mind,' he replied sincerely. 'It's just that I get the third degree from my mother whenever one of them comes in for a check-up.' Jed looked at her. 'Haven't you ever treated a friend of your parents?'

Sally shook her head and looked into her teacup. 'No.' She paused. 'My parents don't *have* friends,' she said matter-of-factly. With that, she stood and took her cup to the sink where she washed it. 'Finished?' she asked him.

He was eyeing her with scepticism. 'No.' He took another sip as if to prove it. She watched him and desperately wanted to know exactly what he was thinking. More importantly, she wanted to know exactly what he thought of her for it appeared that Jed McElroy obviously had some preconceived ideas about her. Although, she quickly reasoned with herself, why did she care? He was just her boss and her supervisor. Nothing more.

'I'd better go and familiarise myself with my consulting room.' With that, she walked out of the kitchen.

Shutting the door to her consulting room, Sally took three deep breaths. She hadn't imagined her new job would cause her so much concern. Well, she thought, it wasn't the job but her boss. A single look from him and a million different emotions zinged through her being without any prompting or control—and it irritated her. If there was one thing Sally liked to be, it was in control—*especially* of her own feelings.

The intercom on her desk buzzed, startling her out of her reverie. Walking across, she depressed the button.

'Yes, Vera?'

'Your first patient is here. Ready for action?'

Sally smiled. 'Ready and waiting.'

The day rapidly progressed and after a quick lunch at her desk, which consisted of fresh sandwiches, fruit and cakes that were delivered daily to the clinic from a mobile bakery, Sally realised she was truly enjoying herself.

Admittedly, she hadn't set eyes on Jed since she'd left him in the kitchen earlier but she wasn't about to dwell on the fact. Vera had brought her in a cup of tea midway through the morning and at the same time taken her lunch order. The patients she'd seen had been very curious about the new doctor but thankfully all had appeared very accepting of her.

'Alice Partridge has finally arrived,' Vera informed Sally via the intercom. They'd been waiting for her almost ten minutes now and Sally had used the time to dictate a few letters.

'Thanks,' Sally replied as she typed in the code for Alice's file. Up it came on her computer screen and she quickly scanned it before going out to get nineteen-year-old Alice.

When Alice was settled in the chair on the opposite side of the desk, Sally introduced herself.

'I'm Dr Bransford.'

'What?' Alice tugged at the zipper on the top of her Institute tracksuit. 'You're *not* a qualified orthopaedic surgeon?' Alice demanded with an arrogant sneer. She flicked her long brown hair back over her shoulder, her brown eyes radiating disdain.

Sally was mildly surprised and forced a smile. 'Yes, I'm qualified, but I just don't fancy being called *Mr*, as male surgeons are.' Her tone was polite and friendly. 'So, what can I help you with?'

'My shoulder is sore—*again*. I need some more anti-inflammatories. I guess I need to explain the whole story to you.' Alice sighed in exasperation. 'Why couldn't I just see Mr McElroy and get a repeat prescription?'

'Actually, Alice, it's *Dr* McElroy as Jed's successfully completed his Ph.D. Regardless of that, I've read your case notes so I *know* the whole story, but why don't you tell me anyway?' Sally urged. She had the distinct impression that there was a lot more wrong here than a sore shoulder.

'I strained the muscles around my right shoulder quite a few months ago,' she recited in a bored tone. 'I've had physio until the cows come home, I've had anti-inflammatories, I've had *everything* but still it's sore.'

'Have you rested it?'

'I had two days off after I initially hurt it and Coach said I'd be fine to continue so I did.' Alice looked down at her hands as she spoke. Sally was picking up more from her body language than anything the teenager was telling her. According to Jed's notes, he, too, was a little worried about Alice and her shoulder.

'When's your next practice session?' Sally asked.

'In about two hours, which is why I need the prescription so I can take some and not feel as much pain as I do now when I practise.'

'Fine.' Sally's smile was still in place. 'If you'd like to get up on the examination couch, I'll take a look.'

Alice rolled her eyes. 'Why do you need to examine me? It's been done before.'

Sally stood and walked over to the examination couch, waiting patiently for Alice. 'Let's just say that I'm something of a specialist when it comes to gymnastic injuries.'

Alice spun around to look at Sally. Sally patted the couch and watched with triumph as the young woman slowly stood and walked over.

'I just want the prescription,' Alice mumbled, but at least complied with Sally's request.

'Please, slowly raise your arm out to the side until your fingers are level with your shoulder.'

Sally watched and knew the precise moment that Alice would wince in pain. 'Good. Now just hold it there for a moment.' Sally noticed that Alice's fist was clenched tightly as she tried to control the pain. 'Turn your palm face up and slowly raise your arm until it's vertical.'

When Alice had complied Sally said, 'Good. Lower it slowly down and rest it. When you're ready, I'd like you to take off your jacket.' Sure enough, as Alice did so, Sally's suspicions were once again confirmed. She wore only a leotard underneath. 'You don't feel the cold?' she queried as she warmed her hands, before placing them on Alice's shoulder.

'No,' came the clipped reply.

'Try and relax.' Sally lightly ran her fingers along Alice's right shoulder, working her way across to the left shoulder, gently applying pressure. 'Your trapezius muscle is as tight as a drum. You mentioned that the physiotherapy doesn't appear to be helping?'

'That's right. Nothing is working. So let me save you some time, *Dr Bransford*—just give me the prescription for anti-inflammatories and I'll be on my way.'

'You've been on them for too long, Alice. I don't want you having any more just yet,' Sally said with concern, before taking a step away from the examination couch. 'Thanks. I'm finished. You can put your top back on now.'

Sally returned to her desk and picked up her phone. She tapped in Vera's extension number. 'Is it possible I can get away in two hours?'

'I thought you'd be asking me that,' Vera replied. 'I can swing it. You want to watch young Alice practise?'

'Yes.'

'I'll make Mrs Marks your last patient, then. She's due at three-thirty this afternoon.'

'Thanks, Vera.'

When Sally had replaced the phone she looked at Alice who was standing by her desk, her arms crossed in front of her, not looking like a happy little gymnast at all.

'You're coming to watch me practise?'

'Yes. I'll see you this afternoon.'

'That's it? You're not going to tell me what's wrong with my shoulder?'

'Not yet. I need to see you in action.'

'So much for a specialist in this field,' Alice snorted, before storming out the door.

Sally typed a brief description into the computer, adding her appointment to watch Alice practise later that afternoon. Once that was done, she was ready for her next patient.

At ten to four, Sally saved all of her files and downloaded them, before switching her computer off. She pressed the intercom buzzer and Vera quickly responded.

'Is Jed free at the moment?'

'I don't think he has any plans to marry in the near future, Sally, but I guess you could always change his mind,' Vera responded with a chuckle.

Sally was glad the other woman wasn't standing in front of her, otherwise her rising colour would have been evident. The way her pulse rate had increased at the mere thought of changing Jed's mind and inducing him to marry her was more than she could handle.

'I...I meant—' she stammered, trying to control her breathlessness before Vera interrupted.

'I know what you meant, Sally. I was just teasing. No, he doesn't have anyone with him at the moment.'

'Thanks,' Sally said, and lifted her finger off the intercom. She collected her bag and coat and walked down the corridor towards Jed's consulting room. Raising her hand to tap on his door, she realised she was shaking with anticipation. 'Stop it,' she whispered to herself. Clenching her fingers tighter into a fist, she knocked forcefully and, not waiting for his reply, she opened the door and took a few steps in. Jed was sitting at his desk, typing on the keyboard with the phone perched between his shoulder and ear. Sally hesitated before his blue gaze snapped up to meet hers.

'Problem?' he asked.

'I'm just leaving now to see Alice Partridge train.'

He grumbled something into the receiver and replaced the phone. 'I suppose you want the keys to my car?' He stopped typing and rummaged around in his top drawer for the keys.

'No,' she replied, instantly on the defensive. 'I can walk. It's not that far to the Institute.'

'But it's cold. What if it starts to rain?'

'Then I'll get wet.' Sally raised her chin defiantly. 'I merely came in here to tell you where I was going. I realise now it was probably a mistake to bother you. Next time, I'll just leave a message with Vera.'

She turned to go but hadn't reached the door before he was by her side.

'Take the car,' he ground out as he grabbed her hand and pressed the keys into it. The touch of his skin on hers sent a spark like electricity shooting up her arm and coursing throughout her entire body. Sally's lips parted as her heart rate, which she'd been working so hard at controlling, shifted into overdrive once more.

Jed's gaze met hers and for a long moment neither of them moved. They simply stared at each other, his hand still holding hers.

Slowly—ever so slowly—Jed's head began to descend towards her own, his gaze never leaving hers. If Sally had thought her breathing fast before, it was nothing compared to now. The tightening in her stomach didn't help either. Jed was about to kiss her! Her mind registered the thought and she instinctively ran her tongue over her lips, wetting them in anticipation.

His car keys slipped through her fingers and clattered to the ground, but still neither of them broke eye contact. Jed's hand tightened around hers and she felt an imperceptible tug on her arm as he urged her to come closer.

She could smell the masculine scent of his cologne as he angled his head, coming closer and closer with such agonising slowness. Sally's gaze broke free of his but only to watch the way his own lips were now parted in expectation of the kiss they were about to share.

Bzzz. 'Jed?' Vera's voice came through the intercom. Sally closed her eyes in pained disbelief. Jed groaned in frustration before dropping her hand and stalking to his desk.

'Yes,' he snapped, not looking at Sally.

She couldn't move. Her body was like a quivering mass of jelly, her legs only barely supporting her.

'Mr Foley has just called to cancel. He's been held up so you're free for the rest of the afternoon.'

'Thank you.'

He looked at Sally. 'Looks as though your chauffeur is available.' His tone was flat and Sally wondered if he was regretting what had just passed between them. So they hadn't actually kissed but the intent was there—was *still* there—between them.

'I'll wait for you at the car,' she said, trying to cover up the huskiness in her voice before forcing her body to move.

Walking quickly down the corridor, Sally said goodbye to Vera and proceeded to the car. She hadn't thought to pick up the keys off the floor before hurrying from Jed's office. All she knew was that she had to get out of there before she all but threw herself into his arms.

She'd known the instant she'd seen Jed that there had been an attraction between them. On discovering his identity, it had only increased as Jordanne had spoken so openly about her big brother Jed for so many years that Sally had respected him long before meeting him.

Although, she surmised as she continued to wait for him, he was completely different from the way Jordanne described him. She'd expected him to be more carefree and fun-loving from what his sister had said but, then, she'd only met him just over twenty-four hours ago. She could hardly classify herself as an expert on Jed McElroy.

She heard his footsteps and looked up. Big mistake. His stride was so confident and purposeful that she wished with all her might that he would come right up to her side and drop his briefcase and coat, before scooping her up into his arms and smothering her mouth with his own.

Instead, he unlocked the car and deposited his things in the boot. Sally opened her door and climbed in, clicking her seat belt closed before he'd even opened the driver's door. Once he was settled he started the engine and without a word drove the short distance to the Institute of Australasian Sport.

It was clear in every movement he made that he had no wish to discuss what had happened between them in his office. He made no attempt at conversation and the defensiveness of his body language prompted the same from Sally. Fair enough, she thought. At least she knew where they stood.

The instant he stopped the car Sally unclipped her seat belt, gathered her things and alighted from the vehicle. She'd stud-

ied the plan of the Institute thoroughly on accepting her position with Jed so that she knew exactly where to go to find
the gymnastics training hall.

Jed watched her go with growing frustration. 'That woman,'
he growled as he climbed out of the car and locked it. If this
was the way their working relationship was going to be, he
wasn't sure he'd be able to survive. Jed raked a hand through
his hair as he followed the path Sally had moments ago taken
to the gymnastics training hall. She was beginning to drive
him insane.

That moment—in his office. He'd known he found her attractive but he'd also thought he'd be able to control his libido
around her. Apparently, he'd been wrong. He'd wanted nothing more than to take her in his arms and kiss her senseless.
In fact, he *still* wanted to do it and it was *that* particular
thought he wasn't at all happy with.

He hadn't been sure what to say when he'd met her at the
car. He was almost positive that she was used to this sort of
thing happening to her all the time—men wanting to kiss her,
that was. She *knew* she was attractive and her wealth probably
made her an even bigger target as far as the single man was
concerned.

The thought struck him quite unawares as he pulled open a
door and walked up a flight of stairs. Sally had been very cool,
calm and collected in the car, even to the point where he'd
thought her rather snobbish, but perhaps it was her way of
protecting herself. She'd no doubt dealt with several fortune-
hunters during her life, although she must know that he wasn't
one of them. *Surely* she knew that. Jed opened another door
and walked along the edge to where Sally was sitting on one
of the benches that surrounded the large hall.

The training apparatus had been built over a large foam pit
that was a storey deep, hence the stairs they'd just come up.
That way, when a gymnast was learning a new routine, if they
fell they wouldn't hurt themselves.

Jed sat down next to Sally—not too close, though. She

didn't even bother to turn and look at him. Instead, she kept her gaze firmly glued to Alice who was busy warming up.

'Excuse me,' a short, balding man said as he walked into the room through a side door. 'What are you doing here?'

Both Sally and Jed turned to face him. He headed over to them.

'This is a private training session.' As he got closer he recognised Jed. 'Oh, sorry, Dr McElroy. Didn't realise it was you.'

'That's all right, Bruce,' Jed replied.

'So…' Bruce gestured to Sally. He smiled at her in a wolfish way, his gaze indicating he liked what he saw. Sally tried not to shudder with repulsion. 'Who's…this?'

'My colleague—Dr Bransford. She's an orthopaedic surgeon who's just joined my practice for the next twelve months,' he explained, with emphasis on Sally's qualifications. 'She'll be taking over Alice's treatment.'

Bruce obviously didn't like this information. 'Oh, will she now? Well, I haven't given my permission.'

'You don't have any choice in the matter,' Jed said with force. 'We'd like to watch Alice train, thank you.' His words were clearly dismissive, and if Bruce had a come-back, he swallowed it.

Sally realised that Jed obviously held quite a bit of clout with the Institute of Australasian Sport if he could hand over a patient's treatment just like that. She turned to look at him as Bruce walked away. 'Thanks,' she said softly and with absolute sincerity.

Once more their gazes held. Sally felt another flutter in her stomach and knew that something strong and powerful was slowly being formed between them.

'You're welcome,' he said eventually, his deep tone washing over her like silk. Sally smiled shyly, before forcing herself to break the moment. She watched as Alice mounted the beam and for a brief second a fierce longing to be back in gymnastic competition pierced her.

She brushed it away as that feeling was followed by the

terrible row she'd had with her parents over her right to choose what she did for a living. She'd won her Olympic gold medal for the beam but that had been seventeen years ago.

Sally bit her lip as she carefully watched every move Alice made. Bruce wasn't a bad coach, from what Sally could see, and to be employed here he was obviously the best in his field. She had to keep reminding herself that she'd trained overseas for her competitions as the Institute hadn't been set up way back then.

'Extend, extend,' she whispered in encouragement as Alice flipped once, twice, three times along the length of the beam. An instant later Bruce called out the same words.

'You're not extending your leg enough, Alice. Again.'

As Alice performed the same routine, she extended her leg more and Sally said, 'Good.'

Alice spun on one leg, her arms extended overhead, before executing a one-handed walk-over. Sally winced. So did Alice. 'See that,' she said, not looking at Jed.

'What? I have no idea what I'm looking for.'

'There!' She pointed triumphantly as Alice contorted her body around the beam, her right arm being her main support. With the angle she was at, it was no wonder the muscles in her arm were being ripped apart. 'That's what's causing the pain. Now, let's see how much the coach exacerbates the situation.'

She felt Jed inch a little closer to her, their thighs almost pressing. The warmth from his body washed over hers and Sally found it even more difficult to concentrate on what Alice was doing. Not daring to look at him, she nearly jumped out of her skin when his breath fanned her neck.

'I'm taking a guess,' he whispered near her ear, 'that you've done gymnastics in the past.'

Goose-bumps ripped down her spine and arms at his words. She swallowed and said automatically, 'Olympic gold medallist for beam.'

'*Olympics?*' he said with incredulity.

'Yes.' She couldn't look at him. She couldn't allow the

closeness of his body to distract her from watching Alice. 'Got a problem with that?'

'No. Merely…astonished. I didn't know.' He was quiet for a second, before asking, 'Why didn't I know that? A lot of previous Olympic stars do advertisements and endorse products, but you don't. Why?'

'I hate publicity,' she replied, still watching Alice.

'Does Jordanne know?'

'Yes, but she knows how I feel about it.' Sally resisted the urge to turn and look at him. 'It was a long time ago, Jed,' she said briskly, indicating she didn't want to discuss it further. 'We all have a past.'

Alice was now sitting on the beam, her legs dangling down like a little girl as Bruce spoke to her. She was massaging her right shoulder with her left hand and rightly so, Sally thought. It must be bad.

'Again,' Bruce called in a loud voice. Sally knew coaches pushed their students hard but couldn't he see that the girl was in pain?

This time as Alice made her way through the routine, Sally watched her more closely than before, knowing the exact time the young woman would wince. When Alice did a backward flip onto her right arm, it came as no surprise to Sally that her right shoulder failed to support her. Her cry of pain came the instant gravity caught up with the athlete and she crashed down onto the beam, before tumbling into the foam pit.

Sally was on her feet and rushing towards Alice before the girl had landed.

'Alice?' Bruce was bending down beside her, concern and guilt on his face.

'Out of the way,' Sally snapped impatiently. 'Let me look at her.' She crouched down next to Alice and carefully felt the shoulder.

'How's it look?' Jed asked from behind her.

'She'll need an X-ray, but I'd say it's dislocated. Can't say more until then.'

'I'll organise analgesics as well as an ambulance,' Jed informed her. 'Stay here, Sally. Be careful in that foam pit.'

She glanced at him over her shoulder and raised her eyebrows.

'Sorry,' he said with a sheepish smile. 'Forgot who I was talking to.' He glanced at the coach who was hovering around like a moth. 'Keep out of her way,' he ordered, before walking out.

'You'll be fine, Alice,' Sally assured her. 'Just try to relax.'

'It hurts,' she insisted between clenched teeth.

'I know. Once you've had some pain relief, you'll feel much better.'

Alice began to sob. 'It hurts, Dr Bransford. It really hurts.'

'I know.'

Jed returned about five minutes later with analgesics. There was a well-stocked medical bay at the Institute which employed two full-time nurses. One of them returned with Jed and administered Alice's injection of pethidine. Once the pain relief began to take effect, Sally was able to check the girl's shoulder more thoroughly.

'Definitely dislocated, but I don't want to put it back in until it's been X-rayed.'

'She…she'll be all right, won't she?' Bruce asked meekly.

'In time,' Sally said pointedly. Another ten minutes passed before the paramedics arrived. The pethidine was helping Alice to cope.

'Why don't you just rest and relax, Alice?' Sally suggested, and received a nod from her patient. As the paramedics tended to Alice, Sally clambered out of the foam pit. 'Has someone notified her parents?'

'No!' Bruce said vehemently. 'Don't…don't tell them just yet.'

'They need to be told, and *now*,' Jed ordered.

'But she's nineteen. You don't need parental consent to treat her,' he pointed out.

'Her parents need to be told,' Jed reiterated. 'They're her next of kin.'

'Her father won't be pleased,' Bruce almost begged.

'What's his name and number?' Sally asked as she watched Alice being transferred to the stretcher.

'Can't we just wait until she's been X-rayed and then we'll know what we're dealing with?' Bruce pleaded.

'Name and number,' Jed ordered, and held out his mobile phone ready to dial in the number.

'Er…' Bruce swallowed. 'Mr…Mr Gordon Partridge.'

Sally did a double take. 'Did you say *Gordon* Partridge?'

'Y-yes,' Bruce replied.

'Know him?' Jed asked.

'Yes.' Sally nodded. 'He's a…business associate of my father's. Huh—it's all beginning to make sense,' she mumbled softly, but Jed heard her.

'What?' he asked curiously.

'I didn't recognise Alice or connect the name, but the last time I saw her she would have been about nine or ten.' She could now understand why Bruce was hesitant to call. Gordon Partridge was as rich and influential as her own father. He crushed people who got in his way and brushed them aside without a second thought. It all made sense. Alice's attitude— her coach pushing her. It was exactly what had happened to Sally when she'd been younger.

'Call him,' she told Jed with determination. 'I'll speak to him.'

Jed dialled in the number Bruce gave and handed the phone over to Sally.

'Mr Partridge's office,' his secretary said. 'May I help you?'

'I'd like to speak to Mr Partridge, please.'

'Is he expecting your call?'

'No.'

'I'm sorry. I can't put you through.'

'My name is Dr Sally Bransford and I'm calling regarding his daughter Alice.'

'I see.' The secretary was obviously curious. 'One moment, please.' Sally listened to the bland music and looked at Bruce who had paled whiter than Alice.

'D-did you say…*Sally* Bransford?'

'Yes.' Here it comes, she thought.

'The *gymnast*?'

'Yes.'

'Your father is…Norman Bransford?' Bruce was getting whiter by the second.

'Yes.'

With her single-word reply, Bruce closed his eyes and keeled over—fainting dead away.

Sally looked with surprise at the man lying in a heap on the floor as the nurse from the Institute knelt down to render assistance. 'Is he all right?' Sally asked with concern as she helped the nurse put him into the coma position.

'He'll be fine,' she replied.

'What caused him to faint?' Jed asked as Sally straightened, the nurse still tending to Bruce.

'Could be anything, but my guess is he's just figured out he might be in trouble.'

'With what?' Jed shrugged, not quite sure what Sally was getting at.

'Well, for starters, as I said, Gordon Partridge is an influential man. He's probably demanded that Bruce make his daughter better than anyone else and possibly threatened him with all sorts of ''you'll never work again if you don't'' scenarios.'

'Give her preferential treatment?' he queried softly.

'Something like that.'

'And what else?'

'Well, the fact that I'm Norman Bransford's daughter and a gold medallist. Bruce would know what happened to me. Sporting gossip is almost as fast as hospital gossip.' She grinned at him. They both looked at Bruce who was starting to come around.

'Anything else?'

'Yes. The fact that as an expert gymnast *and* a doctor, I can quite easily see he's pushing Alice too hard. Not giving the same coaching skills to the other gymnasts could lose him his job.'

'You have that sort of power?'

'I do!'

CHAPTER FOUR

'ARE those X-rays of Alice Partridge's shoulder ready?' Sally asked one of the radiographers who was busy with a bunch of films.

'Should be out any minute,' he replied huffily. 'If you're in such a hurry, go over there...' He pointed to a door. 'Knock and wait for someone to call, "Enter." That's the darkroom. The processing machine has broken down so it's back to the old way for today.' With that, he gathered up an armful of films and walked out.

Sally did as he'd suggested. When she heard a voice telling her to come in, she pushed open the door, only to find it led to a wall. She walked around the little maze that would protect the radiographs in case the door was accidentally opened, squinting her eyes into the darkness.

'Hi,' a cheery female voice called. 'You after the films for Alice Partridge?'

'Yes,' Sally replied, unable to focus clearly on the person who was speaking.

'Put your hand onto the bench, stand still and then close your eyes,' the other woman's voice suggested. Sally did as she was told. 'Right, stay there for a few seconds and then open your eyes. That will help them to adjust.'

'Hey, you're right,' Sally said a few moments later. 'Thanks.'

'I'm Bethany Young,' the other woman said as she moved a film from one chemical tray to another. 'Radiographer extraordinaire.'

'Sally Bransford—new orthopaedic surgeon.'

'Oh, you're with Jed?'

'That's right.' Sally wasn't sure what that comment really meant but it was said in a pleasant tone.

'Welcome to Canberra General Hospital.'

'Thanks.'

'I've known Jed and Alex and the rest of them for years,' Bethany said. Now that Sally's eyes had adjusted completely, she could see Bethany more clearly, lit in the glow of the special red light that was used in darkrooms. She was slightly shorter than herself, had brown hair pulled back into a no-nonsense bun at the base of her neck and large-rimmed glasses surrounded her eyes. Sally guessed she was in her late forties.

'Is that so?' Sally responded politely as Bethany finished fixing the film.

'Yes. We've worked together at several hospitals in Sydney and overseas. Can't seem to get away from either Alex or Jed. One or the other would always be somewhere near.'

'I guess that's kind of nice when you're working overseas and meeting up with people you know.'

'Didn't happen to you?'

'No. When I worked overseas as part of my orthopaedic registrar rotation, I started from scratch. I guess…' Sally hesitated for a moment. 'Never mind. Films ready?'

'Just about.' Bethany fed the film through the dryer, before handing the warm X-ray to Sally.

'Thanks.' Sally held the film up to the red light and peered at it.

'At least we all haven't forgotten how to process films the old way,' Bethany commented. 'This is the second time the new machine has broken down in a matter of months.' Bethany gestured to the X-ray. 'How's it look?'

'Shoulder is definitely dislocated, as well as a fracture to her scapula. How long for the other two X-rays?'

'A few more minutes. Just let me catalogue and label this one before you take it away to discuss with Jed. I'll bring the others around once they're done.'

'Thanks, Bethany. We're in the doctors' tearoom in Emergency—'

'I know where he hangs out,' Bethany said with a smile. 'Get going. Jed hates to be kept waiting.'

'I know. See you soon.'

Sally left, pausing briefly to have a look at the film outside the darkroom. 'Poor Alice,' she muttered.

In the doctors' tearoom, she slid the radiograph onto the viewing box and they both looked at it.

'She'll need a complete shoulder replacement in another five years if she keeps putting the same stress on it,' Jed replied. 'How much longer did Bethany say for the other films?'

'She'll bring them round as soon as they're done.'

'Good.' Jed peered at the X-ray again. 'The fracture to the scapula is quite clean so we'll simply plate it after relocating her shoulder.'

There was a knock on the door and Sister Wildman came in. Sally had met the head orthopaedic nurse when she'd arrived. 'Alice Partridge's parents have arrived and her father is kicking up a storm in A and E.'

'I'm on my way,' Sally said, and strode towards the door. She didn't get far.

'No. I'll talk to them,' Jed replied, reaching out a hand to stop Sally.

The simple touch of his hand on her arm was enough to flood her body with tingles, but she quickly shook the sensation off.

'You have no idea what Gordon Partridge is like. I do.' Sally turned to face him. They stared at each other for a moment, both warring with the other for supremacy. Jed obviously wasn't used to having someone else call the shots, but wasn't that what her job was all about—picking up the slack, taking the pressure off him?

'You never *did* tell me what he said on the phone. I was occupied with Bruce.'

'I didn't speak to him,' Sally replied.

'He was too busy to talk about his daughter?' Jed was surprised.

'You just don't get it, do you?' Sally shook her head sadly.

'She's not his daughter, she's simply a commodity. I just left a message with his secretary that he was to come here because Alice was injured.'

'Then I suppose you hung up?'

'Correct. So if you don't mind, considering the circumstances, I know exactly how to handle Mr Gordon Partridge.'

'I'm in charge,' Jed challenged.

'Go together,' Sister Wildman said in exasperation as neither of them moved. 'Just do something to get that… *man*…out of A and E before the walls start tumbling down in terror.'

'Right.' Jed's jaw was firmly clenched. 'We'll take him to the parents' waiting room and talk to him there.'

'No. Bring him back here.'

'But this is the *doctors'* tearoom.'

'Trust me.' Sally lifted her chin with defiance. Jed had no idea what he was getting himself into. Gordon Partridge had a temper as bad as her father's, and Sally had grown up dealing with forceful and domineering men such as them.

They walked out with Sister Wildman in front, both surgeons ready to do battle.

'I want to speak to the doctor in charge,' a man was blustering, and Sally winced at the tone of his voice.

'Take a breath,' she instructed herself out loud, and Jed shot her a puzzled look.

'Gordon,' Sally said with forced happiness, as she rounded the corner into A and E. 'So nice to see you.' She crossed to his side, using the impact of her unexpected presence to kiss him fondly on the cheek. 'Where's Hillary?' Before he could answer, she'd glanced over his shoulder to where an immaculately dressed woman sat, clutching her handbag as if her life depended on it. 'Oh, there she is. Hello, Hillary,' Sally called, before returning her attention to Gordon.

He wasn't a tall man, was a little bit stout and sported a large grey moustache, the colour matching his hair. His brown eyes had been blazing with rage when she'd rounded the corner but the momentary setback her presence had evoked was slipping quickly.

'Dreadful business about Alice, but I can assure you, Gordon, she's in good hands. Allow me to introduce my colleague, Jed McElroy.'

Gordon ignored Jed's proffered hand and stared at Sally.

'What in the blazes are *you* doing here?' he expostulated. 'I should have known you'd be involved in this somehow. Where's Alice? I demand to see her *now*.'

'Why don't you and Hillary come with me?' She smiled warmly at him. 'I have a private room waiting for you.' With that, she turned on her heel and began walking away, leaving Gordon with no option but to follow her.

'Hillary,' he snapped, and his wife was instantly by his side—just like a well-trained corgi, Sally thought.

'Where's Alice?' he demanded loudly again as they walked along the corridor.

Sally stopped suddenly and turned to face him, a finger on her lips. 'Shh, Gordon. Please, show some consideration for the other patients or we'll have to ask you to leave the hospital.'

'Leave the hospital?' he blustered.

Sally simply glared at him as though he were an insolent child. 'Now, you weren't listening, Gordon, were you?'

'Don't you patronise me, young lady,' he said in a soft tone that was filled with warning.

'That's better.' She smiled and continued on her way. Jed choked on a cough which had sounded suspiciously like a laugh to her. Sally was extremely conscious of Jed watching her every move and she desperately hoped he wouldn't jump in and say anything until they were all securely tucked away in the doctors' tearoom. She could feel him bristling at Gordon's high-handed treatment. The man's refusal to shake hands would have been a big slight to Jed, especially when she knew his feelings on manners and respect.

'In here, Gordon—Hillary,' Sally said as she held the door open for them. 'After you, Jed.'

Once he was inside, she turned to Sister Wildman and said softly, 'Please, don't let us be disturbed.' She smiled at the theatre nurse.

'I'll guard it for you if necessary,' the nurse replied with an affirming nod.

'Thanks.' Sally pulled the door closed. 'Take a breath,' she muttered to herself, before pasting on a smile. 'Tea? Coffee?' she offered, but Gordon wasn't interested in pleasantries and Hillary remained silent.

'Where's my daughter? You can't keep her from me. I know my rights. I'm her guardian. I want her transferred out of this...*public*...hospital and into the finest private hospital Canberra has to offer.'

'All in good time. Alice is fine, Gordon, and actually you're not legally her guardian any more. She *is* nineteen,' Sally pointed out indulgently. 'She's actually having her pre-medication. I believe the intern has explained the operation to you?'

'No one has explained anything.'

'Well, you probably weren't listening carefully enough. My father has the same problem. Nothing to be worried about, but perhaps you should get your hearing checked while you're here.'

'Sally Bransford,' Gordon warned, clearly appalled at her words.

'Calm down, Gordon,' Hillary warned. 'Please, sit down, dear. Listen to what Sally has to say.'

'You've gone too far, Sally, you're being unprofessional,' Jed whispered in her ear.

'You ain't seen nothin' yet.' She wriggled her eyebrows up and down in amusement. She turned her attention back to the Partridges but did a double take as she caught a glimpse of a smile forming on Jed's lips.

'Now, Gordon. As I said, Alice is getting ready to be taken to Theatre. Jed and I will be performing the operation—'

'You'll be doing no such thing,' Gordon objected, and rose from the chair his wife had just convinced him to sit in.

'Oh? So you *don't* want Alice to receive the best treatment? Funny, because I thought you would have. In that case...' Sally turned to face Jed. 'Would you mind paging Alex's junior registrar? I'm sure he'd be available.'

'Not a problem,' Jed replied, and walked over to the phone on the wall. He'd actually picked it up and dialled the numbers before Gordon told him to stop.

Jed replaced the receiver and looked at Sally.

'Can we, please, sit down and discuss this like mature adults who all have one common goal in mind? Alice.' Sally spoke with sincerity and waited.

Gordon slowly sat down. Jed and Sally followed suit.

'Thank you. Alice had a bad fall at her training session today,' Sally began, and told them how she and Jed had been there to watch Alice train.

'Why?' Gordon snapped. 'She's nothing to do with you.'

'I guess it shows just how much faith you have in, first, her coach, and, second, the Institute,' Sally remarked. 'Jed has been the senior consulting orthopaedic surgeon to the Institute for about six years now, and for the past three months Alice has been under his care.'

'And he asked you for your opinion considering you're such an...*expert* on gymnasts, I suppose,' Gordon tried to finish for her. 'Ridiculous if you ask me. You should be taking your rightful place in society as a former Olympic champion. You should have listened to your father,' he pointed out.

'Actually...' Jed spoke to Gordon directly for the first time. 'It was the other way around. I transferred Alice's care over to Sally *because* of her expertise in gymnastics.'

'When Alice presented today with bad shoulder pain, we needed to find out what was actually causing it. We were watching her train when she fell so at least we were able to provide immediate assistance. Right now, however, we need to discuss the surgery we're about to perform.'

There was a knock at the door and Sister Wildman poked her head around.

'X-rays are ready. I also have the case notes for you.'

'Perfect timing,' Sally said and crossed to take the files from her. She went to the viewing box and slid the other radiographs on, illuminating them alongside the one she and Jed had looked at previously.

'Come and take a look.' Sally explained how Alice had fractured her scapula, as well as dislocating her shoulder. 'The scapula is this large, flat, triangular-shaped bone,' she said, bending her arm around to pat her shoulder. 'The neck of the humerus is the ball-shaped end of the upper arm that articulates or rotates within the hollow of the outermost edge of the shoulder.' Sally moved her arm around from the shoulder joint for emphasis.

'What we'll be doing,' Jed continued, 'is to relocate Alice's shoulder, as well as fixing the fracture with a metal plate and a few screws.'

'How soon can she get back to training?' Gordon asked, his previous bluster diminished. The professional businessman was now back in control. After all, Alice was just another business proposition to him.

'Not for at least the next three months.'

'*Three months!*'

Sally had been wrong. His bluster was back with a vengeance.

'She'll require extensive physiotherapy,' Sally added.

'But she'll miss the championships. She's ahead of the entire competition.'

'I'm sorry, Gordon, but that's the way it is.'

'It's not good enough. I need her to be training by the end of next week at the latest.'

'No.' That was all Sally was going to say as she struggled to hold onto her temper. He was just like her father. 'Now, if you don't mind, we need to leave you and get Alice's operation under way.'

'Hold on just a minute. You can't just say no and leave it at that.'

'I just did.'

'I refuse to—'

Sally sighed with boredom. 'The longer you try to argue, the longer you postpone her operation. The sooner she's out of Theatre, the sooner she can start recovering.' Sally collected the casenotes and X-rays as they would need them in Theatre.

'This discussion is by no means over,' Gordon threatened.

'I didn't think otherwise. Now, if you'd like to come with me, you can see Alice before she has her surgery or I can take you to the parents' waiting room.'

'We'll stay here,' Gordon sniffed.

Sally glanced at Hillary who probably wanted to see her daughter but Gordon had put his foot down.

Sally took a breath. 'Unless you're planning on getting medical qualifications, you'll come to the parents' waiting room,' Sally said, forcing a smile.

'Remember,' Jed added, 'we can ask you to leave the hospital, but I'm sure Alice would want you both to be here when she comes out of Recovery.'

'Gordon?' Hillary pleaded, and reached out to take her husband's arm.

'I'm not impressed,' was all he growled. Sally led the way and once Gordon and Hillary were settled in the parents' waiting room, she joined Jed in Theatre. He'd left her to settle Alice's parents while he'd checked on Alice before the general anaesthetic was administered.

'All systems go?' she asked Jed when she joined him at the scrub sink.

'You were brilliant with the Partridges.' It was the first time she'd heard Jed speak with absolute sincerity since meeting him.

Sally bent her head and concentrated on scrubbing her fingernails. 'I've had years of practice.'

'Is your father *really* like that?'

'No.' Sally looked at Jed, meeting his gaze. 'He's worse.' They were silent for a few minutes as both returned to scrubbing. 'Poor little rich girls, eh?' she mumbled, before saying, 'Take a breath.'

'Why do you say that? "Take a breath"?'

'It's what my Russian coach taught me to do. To relax and channel the anger I felt towards my father.'

'Channel it into what?'

'It all depends. Right now, it's channelling it into operating on Alice Partridge so that she'll make an uneventful and complete recovery.'

'And previously?' Jed asked the question so softly that for a second she thought she'd imagined it.

'I didn't graduate as dux for nothing.' The scrub nurse came to assist them so any further conversation was cut short.

They relocated Alice's shoulder back into the socket and after a check X-ray that satisfied both of them that it was indeed back where it belonged, Sally and Jed set to work on plating Alice's scapula.

There was significant muscle and ligament damage around the fracture site where Alice had been complaining of pain. After they'd fixed the plate into position with screws, Jed and Sally fixed a tear in Alice's deltoid muscle and tidied things up a bit.

'That should help with the pain she was feeling,' Sally said as they degowned. 'Although I can't help shake the feeling that…' She trailed off.

'That what?'

'It's nothing. Probably just unfounded suspicions.'

'Tell me,' he said and reached for the case notes before settling down to write them up.

'The ligament and muscle damage would have been caused by repetitive strains.'

'Agreed.'

Sally waited for the penny to drop but it was obvious Jed didn't understand gymnastic training as she did.

'She's a professional, Jed. Repetitive strain?'

His eyes widened as he grasped her meaning. 'Deliberate?'

'No accusations at this stage, but I want to keep a *very* close eye on Alice during the next six weeks while she recovers and especially when she returns to training.'

'Why?'

'You saw the way her father treated her. Where was the fatherly concern and love for his daughter?'

'Attention?'

'I'm not sure it's just for attention. As I said, it's an unfounded suspicion at the moment but—'

'Hi!' Alex Page stopped and came into the tiny area where Sally and Jed were talking. 'I didn't expect to see the two of you here.' He was dressed in theatre garb, just as they were. 'Any news on your car?' Alex asked Sally as Jed continued to write up the operation notes.

'Not yet.' Sally grimaced. 'I'm waiting on a call to let me know the extent of the damage.'

'So how did you enjoy your first operating session at Canberra General?'

'Not bad,' Sally said with a smile.

'Not bad?' Alex raised his eyebrows mockingly.

'Well, the facilities are state of the art but I could have done without operating on the patient.'

'Do you two mind?' Jed growled as he slammed the case notes shut.

'Mind what?' Alex asked.

'Your endless chit-chat while I'm trying to concentrate.'

'Oh,' Alex responded slowly. 'Sorry, mate. Listen, Sally, I've been thinking about our rain check. How about Sunday night? Are you free?'

Sally turned a quizzical glance towards Jed. 'I'll have to check with my boss first,' she responded. 'So, *boss*, am I going to be working on Sunday night as well as Saturday?'

'No,' Jed ground out, before standing and pushing his way between them. 'Do whatever you like.' He turned his back and left them alone.

'What was that all about?' Sally asked, clearly concerned at Jed's behaviour.

'Don't mind him.' Alex's grin was wide. 'So how about Sunday evening?'

'I guess so,' she replied, still worried about Jed's reaction. The man was a paradox. Happy one minute and growling the next. 'Oh, by the way, how is that man we brought in yesterday? Did you find out what his name is?'

'Yes.' Alex nodded. 'His name is Reginald Mulhair and the car he crashed was stolen.'

'Really?' Sally's eyes were wide with amazement.

'Apparently, he and his friends have been wanted for questioning by the police for some time now.'

'The car was stolen?'

'Yes. Reggie was driving it to his mate's house to strip it for parts in order to earn a little cash before his bookie came by to collect.'

Sally's jaw dropped open in disbelief. 'Wow. What a story... And his injuries?'

'Healing nicely. The police are quite pleased about that as it means he can be released from here sooner to face the charges.'

'Does Jed know this?'

'Yes. He called me late yesterday evening to find out.'

'Well, why didn't he say anything?' Sally frowned and shook her head.

'He probably didn't want to worry you. Jed still sees you as sister material and therefore you receive the protective treatment.'

Sally saw red at this. 'Well, I'm not his sister and I don't need protecting,' she responded vehemently. 'Which brings me back to our business dinner. What time?' She made the arrangements with Alex then excused herself to go and deal with Gordon and Hillary Partridge once more.

When she entered the parents' waiting room, Jed was sitting down, explaining how the operation had proceeded. Sally was still a little cross with him for keeping her in the dark about Reggie Mulhair but she listened intently to what he was telling the Partridges.

'She'll be out of Recovery in another half-hour so we'll let you know when you can see her.'

'Thank you,' Hillary murmured politely, but Gordon was less gracious.

'When can she be moved to that private hospital?'

'We'd like her to stay here for a few more days,' Jed answered.

'Now, to our previous discussion. When can she return to training?'

'As Sally explained to you, not for a few months. Alice's ligament, which surrounds the shoulder blade, as well as the muscle tissue was slightly damaged. We've cleaned it up but she'll require further recuperation for this to heal properly. If she risks putting pressure on her shoulder too early—before it's completely recovered—she'll never do gymnastics again. It's that simple.'

Jed's words were said with force and directness, although his tone was still polite. They all waited—Jed, Hillary and Sally—for Gordon's response.

'We'll play it your way for now,' he finally said. 'But I'll be keeping a close eye on her recovery and I warn you—both of you…' he shook a finger at them '…that if *anything* bad happens to my daughter, I'll be taking you both to court.' With that Gordon stormed out of the waiting room with Hillary following close behind him.

Jed stood and walked towards the door before turning to look at Sally. His face was devoid of any emotion. 'Better make sure your malpractice insurance is up to date.'

Those words were the last he spoke to her, apart from the odd monosyllable here and there, for the rest of the week. Alice was indeed transferred to a private hospital within a few days and was making an unremarkable recovery.

Jed still picked Sally up for work every morning and she made sure that she was waiting on the kerb, in the crisp Canberra coolness so that he didn't have to bother getting out of the car. Soothing music played while they drove first to the private hospital to check on Alice before heading towards the consulting rooms. On Wednesday and Friday afternoons, Sally had her salvation in the form of collecting and collating information for her thesis at the Institute of Australasian Sport, which she enjoyed.

The librarian there, Sky, an attractive blonde woman in her late twenties, was an immense help to Sally as she began devouring the resource books available. Sally was able to study all the gymnasts who had come through the Institute's doors and any injuries they'd sustained. It was like manna from heaven and with Jed being so distant towards her, for reasons she couldn't begin to fathom, Sally drew strength from her time away from him.

On Friday night, after Jed had insisted on collecting her from the library to drive her home, Sally had once more thanked him politely for the ride, glad the next day was Saturday and she wouldn't need to see him unless they were called to the hospital for an emergency.

After showering and dressing for bed in warm silk pyjamas, she snuggled up on the couch with a hot mug of herbal tea and reached for the phone. Kirsten answered on the second ring.

'Waiting by the phone?' Sally asked her friend.

'Well, you have been calling me almost every night since you got here.' Kirsten laughed. 'So, how was *he* today?'

'No better. Just the monosyllables.' Sally shook her head and sighed. 'I don't know, Kirsten. Why does it bother me so much?'

'Because he's your boss and you want to make a good impression?' Kirsten suggested. It was the same suggestion she'd offered last night.

'I guess so.'

'You're just settling in to a new job, Sal. Give yourself a bit of time. Soon you'll make new friends and Jed's attitude won't bother you so much.'

'Speaking of which, I've got a date on Sunday.'

'Really?'

Sally could tell Kirsten was extremely surprised. 'Is your mouth hanging open?' Sally asked in jest.

'How did you know? With *whom*? Tell me all the details. I know you attract men like a magnet, but you rarely go out with them. Who is he?'

'Well, it's not a *date*, *per se*, but a business dinner.'

'It's still a night out with someone else. So are you going to tell me or not?'

'Actually, he's Jed's best friend.'

'Aha!' Kirsten said with a hint of triumph in her voice. 'Does Jed know of these plans?'

'Yes. Why?'

'He's probably jealous.'

'*He's not jealous*,' Sally responded with incredulity. 'Jed is just Jed. Sure, he's handsome and good-looking but he's too…moody for me. No. I'm sure Jed doesn't see me as anything other than a colleague.' Sally bit her bottom lip as she remembered that 'almost' kiss in his office earlier on in the week.

'Well, if he's not jealous then what is he?'

'I don't know, which is why I've been calling you all week to try and figure out what I have to do to get my new boss to like me.'

'Why is it so important that he likes you?'

Kirsten and Jordanne had asked Sally similar questions throughout the course of their friendship. They'd come to realise that Sally's upbringing had left a few neuroses hanging around.

'You know why. I don't know, I guess it's a side effect of being a Bransford. I want *everyone* to like me for who I am— not for the money.'

'But Jed hardly knows you,' Kirsten protested. 'You've been working with him for a week. Just give it some time. Now, tell me all about Alex! Is he good-looking?'

'Sure,' she replied half-heartedly.

'You're not interested in him?' Kirsten asked slowly.

'As a friend. He just doesn't…I don't know, ring any bells, I guess. As you said, I need to make new friends and what I've seen of Alex I like.'

'Make sure you lay it on the line, though. Don't go stringing him along.'

'I would *never* string *anyone* along,' Sally replied, a little offended.

'That's not what I meant and you know it. I know you'd never *intentionally* string someone along but you just have a way of causing men to fall all over you.'

'That's not me, that's the money.'

'No,' Kirsten said softly. 'It's you. You're a charming and beautiful woman, Sally, and you've still got a chip the size of Western Australia on your shoulder about your family's wealth. All I'm saying is that as you truly *don't* feel any bells and whistles when you're with Alex, tell him. Be up front.'

'I will,' Sally promised.

Kirsten was silent for a moment before asking, 'Do you feel any bells and whistles when Jed's around?'

'I've told you before, Jed's not interested.'

'That's not what I asked, but I think I just figured out the answer.'

'What are you on about?' Sally asked, even though she knew exactly where Kirsten was going with this.

'You're attracted to Jed. That's why his opinion matters so much to you.'

'I am no—' But Sally couldn't finish the sentence. She knew if she denied the attraction, it would be a lie. She took a calming breath. 'You're right, I am attracted to him. But I thought if I didn't admit it out loud, it would go away. Don't you *dare* tell Jordanne,' Sally warned.

'If that's what you want then I won't, but I'd love to meet Jed again some time.'

Sally frowned. 'I didn't realise you'd met him.'

'It was back in med school. He was working overseas and had returned home for a holiday. Jordanne and I were studying and he was there. No big deal.'

Sally felt that old pang of loss at Kirsten's reminder of their school days. Due to her father's attitude towards her medical training and the fact that he hadn't wanted Sally to pursue it, she'd tried to keep her friends as far away from him as possible. That had meant not getting involved with any of their families in case her father had tried some of the unorthodox tactics he was famous for. So Kirsten and Jordanne had often studied at each other's houses—without Sally. 'Yeah, I remember.'

'Hey, I didn't mean to bring back bad memories,' Kirsten responded, instantly soothing her friend. 'Jordanne and I both knew you'd have loved to have joined us for the study sessions but we also respected *why* you couldn't. After your father offered Jordanne that bribe, we understood *completely* why you wanted to keep us away from him.'

'At least we had some sessions at the library after classes. I don't think I ever would have got through those final exams if it hadn't been for those crazy cramming sessions.' Sally laughed.

'Hear! hear! At least now you're more comfortable in handling your father and can make new friends—like Alex, for instance.'

'That's right,' Sally agreed. It was still very difficult for her to let herself feel free from the clutches of her father. He had ways of finding out things and when she least expected it there he'd be, trying to control her life once more and causing trouble.

'And Jed,' Kirsten pressed.

'Hmm...and Jed. So what did you think of him when you met him all those years ago?'

'Honestly, Sally, I wouldn't be able to pick one of Jordanne's brothers from the other. They all have dark hair and blue eyes. Jed was just one of Jordanne's big brothers.'

An idea sprang into Sally's head. 'Wait a minute. I've just had a great idea.'

'What?'

'Come with us.'

'Come with *whom*, *where*?' Kirsten asked cagily.

'Out with Alex and me.'

'It's a business dinner, Sally.'

'Oh, sure, but we'll talk business for a few minutes and

then that will be over and done with. I'm sure Alex won't mind.'

'But you hardly know him.'

'From what I do know of him, he seems very nice and understanding.'

'Why is it so important that I come?' Kirsten asked, still not committing herself to the idea.

'So you'll be able to see the attraction isn't reciprocated and you can help me get over him before it gets any worse.'

'I thought you weren't interested in Alex?'

'I'm not. So are you free on Sunday evening?'

'Yes, but—'

'Let's make it a double date.'

'Hang on a minute, you want to set me up on a blind date with *Jed*?'

'Why not?'

'Why not? Why is a better question. You've already told me you're attracted to him. What if *I'm* attracted to him, too?'

'You won't be,' Sally said after a moment's hesitation.

'How can you be so certain?'

'One, because you're my friend and, two, when you met him years ago he failed to leave an impression.'

There was silence on the end of the line and Sally knew Kirsten was thinking things through. 'Will you be able to get him to come?'

'I'll get Alex to persuade him. You never know, maybe you'll prefer Alex.'

Kirsten laughed. 'But he's *your*...date, or whatever you want to call it, for the evening. You're not thinking of swapping halfway through, are you?'

Sally grinned into the receiver. 'Anything's possible.'

CHAPTER FIVE

ON SATURDAY night Sally sat around her apartment, waiting for the phone to ring with an emergency. After all, that's what doctors did when they were on call and had no family or new friends and no car. Wasn't it?

At a quarter to ten, just as she was dozing off in front of the television, the telephone shrilled to life.

Sally stretched and reached out a hand for the receiver. 'Dr Bransford,' she replied, hoping she didn't sound sleepy.

'We're on.' It was Jed. 'MVA—two drunk teenagers in a car that was found wrapped around a tree. ETA at the hospital is thirty minutes. I'm in the car, so you have a few minutes to get ready.' His tone was crisp and professional.

'I'll be waiting,' she replied, matching his tone before disconnecting the call. By the time she saw the headlights of his car turn into the court, she was standing on the kerb outside her town house, waiting for him.

Again, there was no communication on the drive between Carella Court and the hospital. Once there, he was barking orders left, right and centre, ensuring that everything was prepared and ready for the arrival of their patients.

Finally, the sirens of the ambulance could be heard. All staff members were at the ready. The instant the ambulance stopped, there were staff everywhere.

'One patient is dead,' one of the paramedics said when the doors were opened. 'A bag of pills was found in the car and this guy's blood alcohol reading was point one four.'

Jed just shook his head in disgust. 'Let's get him inside.'

The patient, complete with oxygen mask and ambulance oximeter, was wheeled inside to the emergency trauma room and transferred to a hospital barouche. Dr Anna Curtis was the intensive care specialist who would be monitoring the patient's respiratory systems. The scribe nurse began writing the patient's details up on a large whiteboard. Sally glanced at the name. 'Jason Delmar,' she said to Jed. 'Fractures to the left femur as well as a compound fracture to his left humerus.'

Jed and Sally inspected the femur, knowing Jason Delmar would require surgery immediately.

'Get that portable X-ray machine over here. I need to see exactly what we're dealing with,' Jed ordered.

The nursing staff had swapped the patient over to a hospital oxygen mask, as well as hooking him up to a hospital oximeter so that the ambulance crews could take their machinery away. The cardiorespiratory monitor was also attached to the patient's chest as Anna Curtis monitored him closely.

As the radiographer began to wheel the X-ray machine towards the patient, a flat-line beep emanated from the cardiorespiratory monitor.

'Defibrillator paddles,' Jed ordered. 'Clear!' Once Jed had administered a shock to the patient's body, the flat line still registered.

'Again. Clear!'

Still nothing.

Jed tried a few more times, increasing the voltage, but to no avail. 'Time of death—twenty-two twenty-five. Myocardial infarction,' he said firmly. He handed the paddles over and looked long and hard at the teenager who had abused his body with drugs and alcohol. 'Have the police notified his parents?' Jed asked, not directing his question to anyone in particular.

'Yes. They're due here soon.'

'Right.'

The atmosphere was one they'd all faced before. Jed wrote up the notes and together he and Sally spoke to the parents of both boys.

When everything was taken care of, Jed collected their coats.

'I'll take you home,' he announced. Sally didn't object. As

an introduction to the on-call roster at Canberra General Hospital, it hadn't been an experience she wanted to savour.

They were both quiet in the car on the way home, which was nothing new but this time it was a shared silence. Jed didn't switch on any music and when they arrived at Sally's town house, instead of waiting for her to get out before he drove off, Jed switched off the engine.

'Fancy some company?'

Sally turned to look at him. His brow was furrowed and his eyes looked tired. 'Sure. Come in for a cuppa.'

'That would be great.'

Neither of them said anything more until they were inside. Sally switched on the heating. 'Shouldn't take too long. Tea or coffee?'

'Tea, please.'

She listed the different types and was surprised when he chose the herbal variety she preferred. 'Have a seat,' she offered as she fluttered around the kitchen. Why was she so nervous that he'd actually decided to come in? Not that she hadn't wanted him to, quite the opposite. All week long Jed's attitude had been building to the stage where she'd found it unbearable. The situation at the hospital tonight had settled a blanket of melancholy over both of them—as though some sort of truce had been called.

After Sally had made the tea they both sat down, Sally on the lounge and Jed in the armchair across the other side of the room.

'Very comfortable,' he murmured as he sat back and stretched his legs.

Sally smiled. She wasn't sure what to say so kept silent. Thankfully, Jed broke the silence first.

'When I was young, just starting high school, I used to hang out with a guy who lived a few blocks away called Davey. He was a laugh a minute and didn't seem to share the reserve that came so naturally to me. Then again, he was an only child and had been indulged his entire life. Mc, on the other hand, I've only had two years without responsibility—my brother

Joel was born when I was two,' he explained. 'Then every two years after that my parents produced another sibling for us to share with. Don't get me wrong, Sally, I enjoyed growing up in a big family, but...' He frowned into his cup. 'The responsibilities have always been there. It became second nature for me to look over my shoulder and call, ''Hurry up!'' when we were walking to and from school, doing a head count to make sure everyone who was supposed to be there was there.

'That's why Davey fascinated me. He made me feel young and carefree—what a boy starting high school *should* feel like. We were good friends until the end of year eleven when his parents took him overseas to visit his cousins in Amsterdam for Christmas. When he returned, he fell in with a different crowd.'

Sally could sense where his story was leading. She tightened her grip on her cup.

'By the middle of that year,' Jed said, his voice lacking emotion, 'Davey was dead. Drug overdose.' He sipped from his cup and looked at Sally. 'I'm sure you have a similar story somewhere—we all seem to. Why? Why do they do it?' He shook his head sadly.

Sally knew his questions were rhetorical and even if they hadn't been, she wouldn't have been able to answer them.

'It's telling the parents that's the worst.' Sally spoke softly after a few minutes.

'You've got that right. I really feel for those parents we spoke to tonight but I'm also so angry with them.'

'I know, but they're probably just as angry with themselves. And unfortunately for them, they're the ones who have to live with it.'

Jed drained his cup. 'Let's not discuss such a dismal topic any more. So tell me—what's the news with your car?'

'Oh,' Sally groaned, and rolled her eyes. 'It's not a write-off and they can repair it—in time. I don't pretend to understand everything the mechanic told me. I guess it's the same as me trying to explain an operation to him. The upshot is that they have to send overseas for some parts so it will be at least a fortnight before the part arrives, *then* they can begin work.' Sally placed her empty cup on the coffee-table and looked down at her hands. 'They've offered me a loan car.'

'You don't need it,' Jed replied. 'It's really no trouble for me to keep driving you.'

Sally looked at him. A look of disbelief. 'You've been as distant as you could possibly be this week, Jed.' She sighed. 'I don't mean that disrespectfully.'

'I apologise,' he replied. 'I've had quite a lot on my mind.'

'You don't need to explain,' she responded quickly, not wanting him to feel bad. 'I just don't want to put you out any more than I already have. I appreciate your help, but if a loan car is available then I think I'll take one.'

'Fair enough.' He nodded and stood. 'When are you picking the car up?'

'Not until Monday afternoon.' Sally followed suit and stood. Jed walked over and picked up his coat and keys.

'I see.'

Sally walked with him to the door. Nervous knots were beginning to form in her stomach at the intimacy of their present scene. She swallowed, trying to get rid of the dryness that had suddenly formed in her throat. She placed one hand on the doorknob and forced a smile.

'So does this mean you'll require a lift tomorrow evening?' he asked in a tone that sounded suspiciously husky. Sally's nervous knots increased. She looked up into his handsome face and met his gaze. The blue eyes were her undoing and she felt her knees begin to buckle. She leaned against the door and thought.

'Lift? Where?'

'For the dinner you've had Alex con me into.'

'Oh, yeah. Alex. Um…' She took a breath and pushed herself away from the door. 'No.'

'No?'

'No, I don't require a lift. Alex said he'd pick me up.'

'But isn't this still a business dinner?'

'Yes,' she said with a frown. 'You pick me up for work. How is this different?'

'Forget it,' he answered with a frown and looked pointedly at the door. 'I'll just pick you up for work on Monday morning, then.'

'Thank you.' Sally smiled up at him but it was as though he was pushing her aside once more.

'Thanks for the tea,' he muttered after she'd opened the door. 'See you tomorrow evening.'

'You'll like Kirsten,' she volunteered.

'I'm sure I shall,' he responded with a wave, before telling her to shut the door to keep the cold out.

Sally wasn't sure how she should take that.

She didn't sleep very well that night and woke around four a.m. from a terrible dream. She'd been at work, talking to Jed about a difficult patient, only it had turned out that the patient had been herself. Jed had diagnosed her as being infatuated with the person she'd been telling him about, and when he'd discovered her secret he'd laughed. Suddenly Kirsten had been at his side and the two had started kissing in front of her. Kirsten had thanked Sally for introducing them. It had been more than Sally could bear. She'd run from the room, tears streaming down her face.

She swung her legs over the side of the bed and sat there for a few moments, before going out to the kitchen to get a drink. She ran her fingers through her hair. 'Whatever happens, happens,' she told herself firmly. 'Your main objective is to relax and have a good time.'

Which is exactly what she told her reflection that evening when she excused herself to go to the ladies room to repair her make-up. Kirsten went with her.

'He's gorgeous,' she told Sally as she took out a small brush and raked it through her long auburn locks. Her green eyes sparkled with delight. 'Just as I remembered.'

'Hmm,' was all Sally said, a frown on her face.

'In fact, I think I'll see Jed again. Quite a catch, really.'

Sally looked sharply at her friend. 'Really?'

'Oh, yes. We've really hit it off, or hadn't you noticed?'

'Yes, I'd noticed,' she grumbled. Alex was a really nice man but, as she'd known since their first meeting, he didn't set off the fireworks—not like Jed. Sally took a deep breath. 'Are you *really* interested in Jed or are you just saying that to annoy me?'

Kirsten shrugged. 'To annoy you,' she said matter-of-factly.

It took a second or two for her words to sink in. 'Really?' Sally asked with hope.

'Yes. Jed McElroy does nothing for me, just as Alex does nothing for you.'

'What about you and Alex?' Sally asked hopefully.

'Nope. Not a thing. Guess I'm not going to meet Mr Right tonight.'

'Sorry,' Sally said sincerely. 'Alex is a real sweetheart.'

'He is but still—nothing. The point is that you *do* feel something for Jed. Stop pussyfooting around and ask him out—just the two of you, *alone*.'

'I don't know, Kirsten. He's so distant at times and yet...' Sally trailed off, unable to put her finger on exactly what was wrong.

'All right,' Kirsten said, holding up her hands in surrender. 'I won't pressure or push you any more, but promise me that if an opportunity presents itself for you to throw yourself into Jed's arms you will take it?'

Sally smiled at her friend. 'I promise.'

'Good. Now, let's get out there and enjoy the rest of our evening.'

'Excellent idea.'

The food was delicious and the four of them had quite a good time. Sally, especially, was able to relax and enjoy herself more after Kirsten's assurance that she felt nothing for Jed. It looked as though her 'nightmare' in the early hours of the morning had simply been her imagination working overtime.

Alex was an entertaining man and openly reminisced how he and Jed had met at med school.

'The first time we met was when Jed's fist connected with my face in a rugby match,' Alex laughed.

Sally raised her eyebrows questioningly at Jed. 'Is this true?'

A slow smile tugged at Jed's lips, his blue eyes twinkling with laughter.

'Absolutely,' he confirmed.

'We were playing for opposing teams and although Jed *claims* it was an accident, I'm still not so sure.' Alex laughed at his own words. 'Regardless, we've remained friends.'

The thought gave Sally an idea. Perhaps she should get Jed to tackle her so they could become friends. The image of him doing just that brought an instant crimson tinge to her cheeks and she bent her head in surprise. Her breathing increased and she could hear her heart pounding. Just *thinking* about the man made her feel all tingly and mushy inside.

'Are you all right, Sally?' Jed asked.

She raised her head to meet his gaze even though her face still felt warm. She swallowed and smiled at him. 'Yes. I'm f...I'm fine,' she faltered. Their gazes held for a second too long and, amazingly enough, Sally saw a burning desire in the depths of his blue eyes. The revelation startled her and she quickly looked away. Jed? Looking at her with...*desire*?

'Is...is there any more tea left?' she asked, not directing her question to anyone in particular. The restaurant had brought out two pots of tea for them to share after their dinner.

'You're in luck, Sally,' Alex said a moment later after he'd checked the pot. 'Might be a bit stewed, though.'

'That's fine.' She waited while Alex poured for her, before adding two large teaspoons of sugar. The sweet, sickly tea snapped her back to reality. She surreptitiously raised her gaze to look at Jed once more as he talked with Kirsten. No sign of the desire there now. She *must* have imagined it.

When they had all finished, it was Jed who made the first move to leave.

'Sally and I had better get going,' he announced. 'Busy clinic tomorrow.'

'Same here,' Kirsten agreed, smothering a yawn. 'The life of a general practitioner seems rather dull after hearing all about your schedule at the hospital tonight, but nevertheless it's what I love.'

'And that's all that matters.' Sally gave her friend a hug and whispered in her ear, 'Thanks for coming.'

'I'm fine to take Sally home,' Alex told Jed.

'It's a bit out of the way for you,' Jed replied.

'No more than you,' Alex countered. 'I brought her here, I'll take her home.' Alex smiled warmly at his friend, and not for the first time Sally realised there was an unspoken communication passing between the two men.

'See you in the morning, Jed,' Sally said. 'I've had a lovely evening.'

'It's been great.' Kirsten nodded. 'We should get together again some time.'

'Great idea,' Alex enthused.

Neither Sally nor Jed commented.

Alex and Sally talked about a variety of things on the drive back to her town house. When they arrived, she invited him in and he accepted. Sally desperately wanted to set him straight, as Kirsten had suggested, and hadn't wanted to do it in the car where they would, no doubt, both have got cold.

Alex declined a drink and sat down in the chair Jed had occupied only the night before.

'Alex,' Sally began in a serious tone.

'That sounds ominous.' He laughed. 'But if you're about to deliver a speech declaring that you feel only friendship for me and nothing more than that, save your breath.'

Sally wasn't sure what to say so she remained quiet and sat down on the lounge.

'You see, I feel only friendship for you as well. No lightning bolts and thunderclaps.'

'Really?' She smiled with surprise. 'That's great.'

'Yeah, it is. By the way, it was a good idea of yours to invite Jed and Kirsten along.'

Sally smiled shyly at the mention of Jed. 'It *was* fun, wasn't it? Thanks for agreeing to stretching our business dinner to accommodate them.'

'As I said when you first suggested it, it wasn't a problem. My main focus in taking new surgical staff out for dinner is to…assess them.'

Sally frowned and Alex continued, 'For example, if a person drinks or smokes a lot, that would be the place they'd do it. Not that there's anything wrong with that, it just lets me know what they're like. I started the dinners when I first became director because my predecessor had a bad drinking problem. So much so that he almost killed a patient in Theatre because he was drunk whilst operating.'

'That's terrible,' Sally gasped.

'Since then I've had one other staff member who had a substance abuse problem. Again, I didn't pick it up just from one dinner but he said a few things during dinner that didn't add up. It was a sign that I should keep a close watch on him and I'm glad I did.'

'So did you learn anything interesting about me tonight?'

Alex smiled as he relaxed into the chair. 'Definitely.'

'What?'

'I learned that you're a very nice person—a person I'm happy to call a colleague and a new friend.'

'Thank you, Alex.' Sally beamed with warmth.

'I learned that Kirsten is searching for Mr Right and didn't consider either Jed or myself candidates.'

'How can you tell that?' Sally asked.

'Body language is a big give-away.'

Sally's eyes grew wide with wonder at his words. 'Anything else?' she asked, now cautious.

'Yes. I noted a thing or two about Jed as well—new developments.'

'What?' Sally was now intrigued.

'You probably won't believe me.'

'Try me.'

'OK.' He hesitated. 'Are you sure you want to know?'

'Yes,' she urged.

'He was jealous of the attention I paid you.'

Sally was stunned. 'Jealous? I don't think so, Alex. I think you read your friend incorrectly.'

Alex's smile increased. 'Exactly the reaction I'd expected. Good. As far as I can see, you're both right on track.'

'Pardon? What are you talking about?'

'If you don't know then I'm not going to tell you.' He stood and fished his car keys out of his pocket. 'Besides...' he added as he walked over to her front door. Sally followed him, still puzzled at his reasoning. 'You're a smart woman, Sally. You'll figure it out.' He bent his head and kissed her cheek. 'I *did* have a great time, though, and Kirsten is right, we should go out again—the four of us. After all, we're all just *friends*. Right?'

With that, he opened the door and walked out. Sally waved goodbye and closed the door, leaning heavily against it.

'Why would Jed be jealous of Alex?' she whispered into the quiet of her town house. 'It just doesn't add up.'

She eyed the phone. It was far too late to call Jordanne and ask if she had any idea of what was going on. 'You're a smart woman...' Alex's words echoed in her head as she changed and got ready for bed.

'If Jed was jealous of Alex,' she reasoned with her pillow, 'then that would mean Jed has feelings for me.' She thought back to that flash of desire she'd seen in his eyes. That, and the kiss they'd almost shared during the week.

'No!' The word was said crisply and she emphatically shook her head. 'Stop being silly. You're hoping to turn fiction into fact.' She blinked into the dark. Alex *must* have the wrong end of the stick. That had to be it.

'But what if...?' she whispered into the night, and closed her eyes to dream once more of Jed. He was becoming way too popular in her dreams and she'd only been working with him for a week.

On Monday when he picked her up for work, he was obviously making an effort to be more talkative. He didn't mention the date at all but rather spoke of an interesting article he'd read in one of the orthopaedic journals. Sally listened attentively, genuinely interested in what he was saying.

When Jed brought the car to a stop in the car park, he removed his sunglasses and was about to put them in their case when he fumbled with them. They dropped between the seats and he reached his hand down to collect them just as Sally went to unclip her seat belt.

Their hands collided and both looked up, startled at the contact. Sally jerked her hand back, as though burnt. The mere touch from the warmth of his skin had sent a rampage of tingles that burst instantly throughout her being, flooding it with desire. Her gaze was wide with wonder and she sucked in a breath.

'Sorry,' she mumbled with a small smile as she desperately tried to recover her equilibrium.

Jed's gaze never left her own and she watched as his brow creased into a frown at her actions. Sally's smile disappeared. Why was he frowning?

'Jed?'

His response was to turn from her and open the door. He'd collected his briefcase and coat and was heading for the stairs before Sally had even alighted from the car. She headed after him.

'Jed?' she called again, her voice more certain. He didn't stop. She rushed after him and managed to catch up with him in the corridor outside her office.

'Please, stop,' she implored.

He turned slowly to look at her.

'Jed? What's wrong?'

'Nothing.'

'I don't believe you.'

The phone in his office began to ring and he glanced down the corridor. 'I have to answer that,' he responded, and stalked away from her.

Sally entered her own office and hung up her coat. 'The man is an enigma,' she told the room. 'One I don't think I have a chance of understanding.'

Both she and Jed, as though by unspoken mutual consent, adopted a professional attitude towards each other. Sally enjoyed her research sessions at the Institute, interviewing athletes and watching them train. Bruce, when she saw him, was polite and courteous but never mentioned one word about Alice Partridge or her recovery.

Sally checked up on Alice once a day and often stayed around to chat. Slowly but surely the teenager was starting to open up and it was what Sally had been hoping for.

'When can I go home?' Alice asked the following Friday.

'You ask me that every day, Alice,' Sally replied with a large smile. She was sitting in the chair next to Alice's bed after giving her a check-up and reading the nursing notes.

'Perhaps it's because I don't like your answer,' Alice ventured. The words were said with a small smile and Sally was reassured once again that she was making progress.

'You have everything you want right here. Your father has paid for the best possible hospital care and in your own private room which, I might add, looks just like a five-star hotel room. You shouldn't have cause to complain.'

'Surely *you* of all people knows what it's like.'

Sally looked at Alice and nodded slowly. 'Who told you?'

'Who's telling who what and why don't I know about it?' a deep male voice asked from the doorway. Both Alice and Sally turned to see Jed lounging there, his hands in his trouser pockets.

'Jed!' Sally said, and stood up. She couldn't ask what he was doing here because it was obvious.

'I think this is the first time our visits have coincided,' he remarked to Sally as he crossed to the foot of Alice's bed and checked her chart. 'Good progress, Ms Partridge.' He nodded. 'Keep it up. How's the operation site?'

Alice glanced at Sally as Jed checked the wound site, pronouncing himself satisfied. When he was finished he sat at the foot of Alice's bed and looked at both women.

'Don't let me intrude on your conversation,' he announced.

'Who told Alice what?' he asked Sally, his eyebrows raised in deliberate interest.

'About who I am,' Sally said slowly.

'Oh.' He nodded as though he completely understood. 'The gold medal.'

'Can you believe it?' Alice asked him, completely amazed. 'A gold medal gymnast is now my orthopaedic surgeon. Cool, if you ask me.'

'So what else do you know?' he asked Alice.

Sally wasn't sure how she felt about him intruding on the time she spent with Alice. She was trying to save this girl from a fate worse than death—that of being controlled by a dominant man for the rest of her life. Jed would *never* understand.

'That her father is a business colleague of my father's.' It was obvious he wasn't going to leave and that Alice wanted to talk about things. Sally sighed and settled back into the chair. 'Have we met before?' Alice asked Sally.

'Once, as far as I can remember. You were about nine or ten.'

'I don't remember.'

'It was at a Christmas function. It's not that important.' She waved her hand in the air in a dismissive gesture. 'So how did you find out?'

'My mother,' Alice said, and studied her hands. 'Usually my father won't leave us alone to talk for fear that we might plot a rebellion against him,' she said with a nervous laugh. Sally knew her words probably weren't far from the truth. 'But the other night he was on an important call. I was dozing, or at least pretending to so I wouldn't have to talk to him. That's when Mum told me who you were. She said that if anyone could help me, you could. That was all she could say as he came back into the room. They left immediately. I did some checking with the Institute librarian who was just as surprised as me at your *true identity*.'

Sally nodded. 'That would explain Sky's attitude towards

me the other day when I was in there. She kept smiling secretly.'

'Does it matter?'

'No. It's just a part of my life that…' She hesitated, aware that Jed was hanging on every word '…well, I guess that I don't like to advertise.'

'Why not?' Alice asked.

Sally sighed. 'Are you sure you want to hear this? I don't want you to feel as though I'm influencing you with what happened to me, because it's quite similar.'

'Please?' Alice settled back amongst the pillows as best she could.

Sally glanced at Jed and he smiled at her, encouraging her. *He* wanted to hear it as well. His eyes twinkled when he smiled like that and erased the normally harsh lines she'd grown used to seeing. She took a breath and began.

'It was my father's idea for me to pursue a sport and become the very best. After all, only the best is ever good enough for him, and even then there are some occasions when he demands more. I loved watching gymnastics so that's what I chose. The fact that I'm taller than most gymnasts was against me from the start, but I knew that if I simply concentrated, I could do it. I actually loved it at first, but by the time I reached the higher competitive levels, such as the World Championships and the Olympics, I'd had enough. Not so my father.' Sally shook her head sadly. 'I trained in Russia under the tutelage and guidance of the, well back then, world's best coach. She taught me so much about life and how to focus my anger towards my father.

'Finally I could endure his demands for perfection no more. I was doing the best I could. I was winning everything but he desperately wanted the gold medal in the Olympics. My coach argued with him that I was being pushed too hard and he fired her, placing me under the care of someone he could control. My training programme was rigorous, and at one stage I was hospitalised from exhaustion. That was two weeks before the Olympics. My father was furious.

'He flew to see me. He was adamant that I win or he would pull his sponsorship of the Australian team and, believe me, it was a lot of money he was investing. I was seventeen and finally decided that enough was enough.'

'What did you do?' Alice's eyes were as wide as saucers at Sally's tale.

'I cut a deal with him. If I won the gold, he would let me choose my own career. If I didn't, then he would decide my next move.'

'Wow! What a gamble. Were you scared?'

'Of losing or my father? I'm not sure which I feared more, but I was desperate. I was also good—*very* good. I knew the competition and I knew I could beat them.'

'And you did.'

'Yes.' The word was a determined reminder of how Sally had gained her independence from her father. 'I won the gold and decided to study medicine. With all the training I had done, my school work needed a bit of polishing. Even then, I managed to make the grade to be accepted into med school.'

'And your father has never bothered you since.' Alice sighed as though this was an impossible dream.

'I wish that were true. No.' Sally shook her head slightly. 'He still attempts to control my life by offering money to hospitals where I've applied for jobs so that they'll take me. I've even turned down positions because I knew I wasn't being accepted on my own merits.'

'That must have been difficult.'

'I had to take a stand,' Sally explained. 'I still need to. He insisted on paying for my medical schooling as part of our deal and I accepted, but the instant I passed my medical exams I started living off my own money. It wasn't easy to begin with as an intern's pay really isn't much, but I learned to cope, and with the help of good friends I'm where I am today.'

They were all silent for a while. 'Do you miss it? The training, I mean,' Alice asked quietly.

'Yes and no. I miss the passion I used to feel for the sport before my father killed it with his outrageous demands. Now

I love medicine, and being able to finally combine the two aspects—medicine with gymnastics—I'm happy.' As Sally spoke, tears misted her eyes. 'I'm finally happy,' she whispered. 'Please,' she implored, 'don't wait as long as I have to find happiness. If you're not happy doing gymnastics, Alice, don't let your father or anyone else stand in your way of leaving.'

Alice's bottom lip began to tremble. 'If I leave…what will I do then?' Alice whispered.

Sally clutched at Alice's left hand. 'Anything you choose,' she replied with sincerity.

Tears welled in the young girl's eyes and tipped over her lashes to roll down her cheeks. Sally reached for a tissue and handed it to Alice.

'What is it?' she whispered. 'Anything you say is held in the strictest confidence,' Sally assured her.

Jed nodded and crossed to the door to close it.

Alice sniffed and sucked in a shaky breath. 'I've been…' She swallowed and tried again. 'I've been doing the routine wrong on purpose,' she blurted, and then went on with a rush, 'I knew it would hurt my shoulder and that finally I'd be allowed to stop training.' The tears rushed forth as Alice sobbed. '*No one* was listening to me. *No one* was taking any notice when I said I was tired or fed up. They just kept pushing and pushing—' Alice broke off and Sally embraced her, letting her patient cry her frustrations and exasperations out.

'I know, I know,' Sally crooned. Her gaze met Jed's and locked for a moment. She was glad he'd stayed, glad he was here to offer his support to Alice as well.

'I didn't know it would be this bad,' Alice said after a while, hiccuping as the tears subsided.

'I know,' Sally repeated as Alice gently pulled away.

The gymnast looked at Sally for a brief second before saying, 'Yes, you *do* know, don't you? You knew when you examined me that the injury might have been done on purpose.'

'I had a suspicion,' Sally admitted. 'It's irrelevant now.

What's important is that while you're recuperating think about what it is that you *really* want to do. When are you the happiest? Let's turn a negative into a positive. Whether or not you compete again is up to you, but your shoulder still needs to heal properly.' Sally finished her spiel by checking Alice's pulse rate. Normal.

'Thanks, both of you, for being here and not making me feel stupid.'

'You're *not* stupid,' Jed responded with a little force. 'Admitting what you did took a lot of guts. I'm proud of you,' he finished with a gentle smile.

Alice blushed slightly at his attention, before looking at Sally. 'What you've said tonight means a lot.'

'I'm glad I could help and, regardless of what you decide, Alice, remember you can always come to me if you need a friend.'

Once more they were all silent. Sally let go of Alice's hand and sat down again. She slowly raised her gaze to meet Jed's. He was looking at her with a mixture of admiration and surprise.

'My mother is another problem,' Alice blurted out after a pause. 'She's weak and lets him trample all over her feelings. Sometimes I despise her for her weakness and then I feel I'm more like my father than I realise.'

'I know,' Sally sympathised. 'Our mothers are caught in a time warp. I love my mother,' Sally said with a smile. 'I also know she honours and respects her husband in a way I can't understand. Equal partners, that's what I'll be demanding when I get married.' She purposely didn't look at Jed as she said the words. She felt very self-conscious but knew she had to push it aside in order to get her point across to Alice.

'I also know that, regardless of how my father treats her, deep down he does care about her. She, on the other hand, adores him. She'll forgive him the world and do his bidding. He never hits or abuses her—he just, in my opinion, belittles her. As far as he's concerned, women are the inferior sex.' Sally shrugged. 'Mum's happy with the way things are and I learned long ago to stay out of their relationship. She's a grown woman.'

Alice nodded emphatically, completely agreeing with everything Sally said.

'You're strong, Alice. You have guts and staying power. If you didn't, you wouldn't have made it to the Institute.'

'No, I'm not strong,' Alice said between clenched teeth. She lifted her head and looked first at Jed and then at Sally. 'My father bought my way in. Make a sizeable donation and they'll take his daughter.'

'No.' Sally shook her head. 'I've seen you train, remember, and I know brilliance when I see it. You're good, Alice. *Very* good. You have the opportunity to win gold as well, and if there's one thing we both seem to have inherited, it is our fathers' will power. He may have bought your way in, but now that you're there, use it—use it for *you*. For what *you* want to accomplish.'

Sally's pager began to beep but she ignored it. 'I should warn you that when your father finds out about this conversation, as I'm sure he will because men like him have a way of discovering these things, you can guess what his reaction will be. But remember, this is *your* life. Please, don't allow him to ruin it.'

'I won't,' Alice replied with force, lifting her chin a little higher with defiance.

CHAPTER SIX

JED was silent when they left Alice's room and walked towards the car park. Sally was warm in her coat but left her gloves off as she couldn't drive with them on. Therefore, she was surprised when her coolish hand was taken firmly in Jed's warm one.

He didn't say anything. He simply held her hand as they made their way through the car park. Sally was touched at his thoughtfulness, and although she was aware of the way her heart rate increased she knew it was merely a friendly gesture.

His Jaguar was parked next to the Mazda 323 she'd been given as a loan car. When they stopped beside the cars, he gave her hand a little squeeze and let it go.

'Thank you,' he said, and bent his head to kiss her cheek. He pulled back quickly and smiled at her, the smile not reaching his eyes. 'I appreciate you allowing me to stay and hear about your past.'

'As I said to Alice, it's no big secret, it's just...' she paused '...not my life any more.' She looked up into his eyes and smiled. 'Thanks for being there. I'm glad you know.'

Jed looked away into the darkness of the night that had enveloped the city whilst they'd been inside the hospital. 'It's late,' he commented, and returned his gaze to meet hers.

Sally nodded. Even if she'd wanted to speak, she didn't think she'd have been capable, with Jed's close proximity, those sexy blue eyes, the warmth of his body not too far away from her own. She took a step back and leaned against her car.

'Would you like to have dinner with me tonight? Just as friends,' he added quickly.

93

Sally beamed up at him and nodded again. 'I'd *love* to have dinner with you.'

Jed shoved his hands into his pockets as though he was trying to stop himself from touching her. She wished he would!

'Why don't you follow me? I know a great place where the food is superb and it's nice and quiet.'

'Sounds good.'

Sally's excitement increased as she followed Jed's tail lights, making sure she didn't lose him. An evening alone—with *Jed*. Perhaps this was it. Perhaps tonight they could build a firmer foundation for a relationship—one not *solely* based on friendship.

As they wound their way passed the Institute and the clinic, Sally frowned. She hadn't heard of any restaurants down this end of town. This was a residential area. Nevertheless, she continued to follow him. When he pulled into the driveway of a house, she instinctively knew it was his.

'Well,' she told herself out loud, 'this is even better than I'd planned.' It had started raining on the drive from the hospital, so Sally parked in the driveway behind Jed's car and made a mad dash for the garage where he was waiting for her.

'Come through this way.' Jed led her through the back entrance of his home. 'Sorry, it's a bit of a mess,' he apologised, motioning to the kitchen. 'I was working late last night and was too tired to clean up.'

'Don't apologise,' Sally said quickly. 'What were you working on?'

'I need to apply for funding for new equipment for the biodome at the Institute. We need two more specialised cameras as well as at least three more machines to monitor the athletes' vital signs.'

They talked more about the biodome and how impressive it was while Jed quickly stacked the dishwasher, cleaning the kitchen in no time.

'So, what delights are you going to make for me this evening?' Sally asked as she settled down on a bench stool to

watch him. He looked good in the kitchen, so sure of himself.
Perhaps it was because she'd never really *seen* a man in a
kitchen before, knowing that her father thought any domestic
task was completely beneath him. She'd been raised with servants and nannies to care for her every need.

'Do you like Thai?'

'Yes. It's my favourite. You can cook Thai?'

'It's not that difficult,' he responded.

'I'm sure it is and that you're just being modest.'

Jed laughed. A rich sound that filled Sally's heart with
warmth. This was the first time since her arrival that he was
allowing her to see the real him. His laughter made her smile
increase.

'Flattery will get you everywhere,' he responded, and began
taking things out of cupboards and the fridge.

Before her very eyes, Jed produced a dish that was not only
colourful to look at but was healthy, too. Sally laid the table
and soon they were ready to eat.

'Wow!' Sally savoured a mouthful. 'When you told me you
enjoyed cooking, I had no idea it was anything like *this*. It's
incredible, Jed.'

'Thank you.'

They talked on a variety of topics but it wasn't until they
were enjoying a hot cup of tea that Jed mentioned Sally's past.

'It must have been hard, growing up with a domineering
man as a father.'

'I guess I didn't know any better until it was too late. My
father was rarely around when I was young but the nannies
who raised me were under his strict orders of what to do and
not to do.'

'And your mother?'

'Charity work. She's involved in a number of charities that
take up a lot of her time. I saw her daily, though. She'd stop
by in the afternoon and spend an hour with me, either reading
books or helping me with my homework. As I said, I love her
dearly but I can't for the life of me understand why she's
attracted to someone like my father.'

'No siblings?'

'No. My mother is very slight and she almost died having me. The doctor advised no more children.'

'I can't imagine what it would have been like, growing up without children all over the place. There was never a moment's peace in our household.'

'Sounds nice.'

'Yeah. Seeing it from your perspective, I guess it does sound nice.'

Their gazes held across the table and Sally sighed. 'You have a lovely home.'

'I wish I could take the credit for it but my sister, Jasmine, loves to decorate and she was simply itching to get her hands on this place.' He shrugged. 'How could I possibly refuse her? She did the entire house—except the study.'

'Is she a decorator by trade?'

'No. She's the mother of four children and has a strong interest in decorating.'

'I remember Jordanne telling me. Two sets of twins—is that right?'

'Yes.'

'But none of you are twins.'

'No. My mother had six separate pregnancies and six healthy babies.'

'She must be quite a woman.'

'She is. You've never met her?'

'No. I've only met Jared—he's the youngest, isn't he?'

'Yes. When was that?'

'At least ten years ago, if not more. It wasn't long after I'd met Jordanne.' Sally waved the memory away, hoping he wouldn't dwell on it. He must have known that her father had offered Jordanne money in exchange for her friend's help in talking Sally out of going to med school. She looked up at him and read the expression in his eyes. Yes, he was thinking exactly the same thing she was. Sally held her breath, waiting for him to speak.

'Well, you'll have the chance to meet all of them soon.'

Sally's breath rushed out at his words and heart rate zapped into the faster pace once more. 'Pardon?'

Jed gave her a wry grin. 'My mother's insisting on throwing me a birthday party. It's at the end of next week. Hopefully your invitation is sitting at home in your mailbox, waiting for you.'

Jed was inviting her to his birthday party. Hopefully *that* meant something! 'I see,' she said slowly. 'So when is your actual birthday and how old will you be?'

'A week from today and I'll be forty-two.'

Sally smiled, pleased he'd been forthcoming with the information. She etched the date into her memory.

'No age jokes, please. I get them constantly from my brothers and sisters.'

'I wasn't going to say a thing.' Her smile increased. 'Any specific occasion for the party?'

'I was away last year and for my fortieth. I think Mum would have disowned me if I'd been away again this year.'

'Conferences?' Sally asked.

'Exactly. Alex is representing the hospital this year so unfortunately he won't be attending my party.' Jed didn't sound too disappointed, she noted. Something was definitely going on between the two friends but she wasn't sure what.

'I look forward to receiving the invitation.'

Neither of them said anything for a few minutes, the silence growing between them.

'So…' Sally cleared her throat. 'What's so special about your study? Why didn't Jasmine decorate that, too?'

Jed merely smiled at her words.

'Are you hiding some deep, dark secret?' Sally's eyes were wide with excitement. She rose from the table.

'What makes you ask that?' He laughed as he looked up at her.

'Show me…please?' She held out her hand to him and slowly, almost reluctantly, he stood. Reaching out, he slid his fingers into hers and grasped them tightly.

'This way.'

Sally's arm was flooded with tingles at his touch before the sensation spread like wildfire throughout her body. She exhaled quietly as she was led down the hallway. He stopped outside a door, opened it and flicked the light switch on. The room was warm from the ducted heating and he guided her inside. Sally gazed around, taking in the very masculine feel of the room.

Bookshelves, filled to the brim with books, lined the walls on two sides. Jed's large Australian jarrah desk occupied another. A framed photo of his family sat on the right of his desk and the rest of the space was cluttered with papers. Sally's mouth twitched with a smile. His desk at work was always so immaculate. She was glad to see he let sloppiness reign *somewhere*.

But it was the half-dozen framed seafaring maps adorning the two bare walls that interested her most. She took a step closer, breaking the contact.

'Are these...original hand-drawn maps?'

'Yes.'

Sally was amazed at the detail. They were all of the Australian coast, or at least different parts of it. 'These are incredible.' Sally glanced over her shoulder at him. 'Do you collect them or were they a present?'

'I collect them,' he answered. 'I keep my ear to the ground and when one comes up I'm interested in, I check it out.'

Jed reached out a hand to straighten one of the frames, but as he did his arm brushed against Sally's shoulder and the pilot light she'd been attempting to keep under control burst forth into a white-hot, searing flame and she gasped with delight. She turned quickly to look at him, his hand dropping to his side, the task abandoned. His blue gaze met hers and the close proximity of the room became even more intimate.

Sally watched as Jed swallowed before her gaze stayed on his lips, knowing they'd bring her to life with only the slightest touch.

He cleared his throat. 'More...tea?' Jed took a step away and Sally's heart sagged with disappointment.

Before she could reply, he'd turned and walked out of the study, leaving her to follow. She took one last look around the room, marvelling at how 'him' it really was before turning off the light and closing the door.

Jed was standing at the sink, rinsing out the teapot. Sally sat back down at the table, watching him go through the motions. When he was finally seated, with two fresh cups of tea before them, she took a breath and summoned up the courage to ask Jed the question which had been burning within her since the day they'd met.

'Jed?'

'Yes?'

'Do you...? I mean...is there...something about me that you find offensive? I only ask because you've been...well, distant with me since we first met.'

Jed looked down into his cup thoughtfully before raising his gaze to meet hers. 'I guess, in a way, that the answer is yes.'

'I see,' Sally recoiled as though she'd been slapped. She'd been expecting him to say that she'd been imagining things. She recovered quickly. 'What is it? Please, tell me.'

'I feel ashamed of my behaviour now—especially after what you told Alice tonight.'

'I don't follow.'

'Wealth, Sally. I have a general dislike of wealthy people who believe they can buy anyone off. They think that because they have money that "normal" people are beneath them—inferior. I've met the Gordon Partridges of this world too many times not to know their type when I see them. You're from a wealthy background so I was...' he searched for the right word '...cautious around you. I know what happened between your father and Jordanne.'

She nodded, indicating she knew there were no secrets in their family. 'There's something more, though. Something you're just not telling me.' She waited another few moments, and when he didn't speak she ventured, 'It's all right. I don't expect you to tell me. I have no intention of prying but if it's OK with you, I'd like to continue with our...friendship as we've been tonight. You know, talking openly and communicating and not just about medical things.'

Jed shook his head. 'I want to tell you what happened to me. It was a long time ago but the scars are still there.' He took a steadying breath. 'Ten years ago, I had a patient by the name of Anya Tolstoy. Heard of her?'

'The Tolstoy Conglomerate? I've heard of them.'

'That's the one. Anya was involved in a terrible car accident and spent quite a bit of time in hospital recovering. We fell in love and started dating. She was studying at university then. Things became quite serious, we even started making wedding plans. I had no idea who her parents were. She'd always been evasive and didn't want to discuss them. Needless to say, we never met. Eventually, Anya was summoned home only to find that her father had arranged her marriage. It was part and parcel of a billion-dollar merger. When Anya said she wouldn't go through with it because she was in love with me, her father attempted to buy me off. He came to see me and tried, for hours, to persuade me to reject his daughter. I refused.

'I didn't see or hear from Anya for a week. I was going out of my mind with worry. Then one morning I picked up a paper and there was her picture. She'd been married to the man her father had chosen. I don't know what he did to her but the game was played his way.'

Sally was silent. She knew all too well how manipulative men like her father were and the Tolstoy Conglomerate was a huge business. They had their fingers in a lot of pies—media, pharmaceutical companies, *hospitals*. Sally had no doubt that Anya had been blackmailed with Jed's professional welfare.

'As I said, it was a long time ago but hearing you talk tonight brought a lot of those angry emotions back. I apologise for my behaviour to you during the past weeks, only offering in my defence that I was being cautious.'

'Have you seen Anya since?'

'Yes, actually. I bumped into her at a charity ball for cancer research about two years ago. It was quite surprising. I hardly recognised her. She was cool and professional towards me and...' Jed shook his head '...I felt no spark of desire or anything. The feelings I'd had for her were well and truly dead, while the anger over what her father did still runs quite deep, as has been proven by our...strained friendship.'

'I hope that can all change from tonight.' Sally stood from the table and carried the teacups over to the dishwasher. 'Thanks for telling me about her.'

'Thanks for listening.' He brought the teapot and sugar over to the sink. 'I feel as though a weight has been lifted from my shoulders.'

Sally placed her hands on his shoulders. 'I'm glad.' Her smile was radiant as she looked up into his face. 'They're broad but they carry way too much on them,' she jested. 'Jordanne's told me how you constantly worry over the rest of your siblings.'

'It's a hard habit to break.' His voice was husky and Sally suddenly realised how close they were in the confined space of his kitchen. She went to remove her hands from his shoulders but Jed stilled their movement, drawing her closer and placing her arms about his neck.

Next he twined his arms around her waist, urging her even closer still. His head started its descent as her lips parted in anticipation. When his lips finally met hers, Sally gasped in wonderment before melting into his embrace, matching the same slow and gentle pace of his mouth.

His kiss was tantalising and sensual and Sally felt her knees begin to buckle from the onslaught of emotions he was evoking. Jed merely picked her up as though she weighed next to nothing and lifted her onto the bench, their lips never breaking contact.

Sally sighed into the kiss as he stood in front of her, his chest pressed firmly against her own. She laced her fingers through his hair, holding his head in place just in case he decided to end the sweet and pleasurable torture she was experiencing.

His tongue gently prised her lips further apart and as he deepened the kiss the emotions that were coursing hot and hungry throughout Sally's body now burst into flames. Her feelings were so intense, she thought she might pass out from the euphoria.

Jed placed a hand on either side of her face and kissed her once, twice, three times before gently drawing away, his breathing as hard and heavy as her own.

'Sally.' Her name was a caress on his lips as he looked down into her face and smiled. His blue eyes were dazed with passion that she knew matched her own. 'Sally,' he said more normally, and she watched as he suddenly looked alarmed. *'Sally!'* He took two steps back from her and turned around. 'What have I done?' he groaned and raked a hand through his hair.

'Jed?' she asked, completely bewildered. 'What? What do you mean, ''What have I done?'''

He turned to face her. 'Alex. He's my best friend. How could I do this to him?'

Before she could ask another question, about what Alex had to do with anything, the phone rang. Jed snatched it up instantly.

'Jed McElroy,' he barked into the receiver.

Sally slid down off the bench and straightened her clothes.

'When?' She watched as he frowned and checked the clock. 'Thanks. I'll be there soon.'

'Elena Marks,' he announced. 'You would have seen her last week in the clinic.'

'I remember,' she responded as she watched him gather his coat and keys. Obviously, they were about to leave. Sally followed his example.

'She's fallen in her bathroom and fractured her wrist and arm, as well as some toes. She's already at Canberra General, being X-rayed, but as she's a private patient we've been called in. Got everything?' He didn't wait for her to answer. 'Let's go.'

Sally tried hard to freeze the moment where she and Jed had left off before the phone call. After a kiss like that she wasn't going to let anything get in her way of finding out exactly what he'd meant when he'd started babbling on about Alex.

They took their separate cars to the hospital, and when they arrived Mrs Marks had just finished in Radiology and the anaesthetist was administering the pre-med.

Jed spoke with her while Sally went into the female changing rooms to get ready. The next time she saw him was at the scrub sink.

'How do the X-rays look?'

'Not too bad. Left Colles' fracture, which we can fix with Plaster of Paris, left radius and ulna will require open reduction and internal fixation with plates and screws. The toes we'll strap. Coccyx is bruised but no further damage.'

'Good.'

The operation proceeded without complication and Sally concentrated on assisting Jed as they debrided the radius and ulna wound site before plating the broken bones back into place. When they were both satisfied with the condition of the arm, Jed closed the wound in layers before they turned their attention to the wrist.

Afterwards, Jed sat down to write up the operation notes in the doctors' tearoom. 'This fall is going to give Mrs Marks's family another point against her, I'm afraid.'

Sally nodded thoughtfully. 'I read her notes when she came to see me last week. I know her husband died some years ago and she's on her own, but what's the rest of the story?'

'Her children want to put her in a nursing home and sell the family property. I've already had one of her sons come to see me, hoping to convince me that his mother was completely senile and was a risk to herself if she was left living alone. He wanted me to testify to it.'

'Why?'

'Both sons, from what I gather, are heavily in debt.'

'So if they sell the family home, it should help pay off their debts,' Sally reasoned. 'It all makes perfect sense to them. Mum's old, the house is too big for her. Let's stick her in a nursing home and collect the money.'

'Exactly.'

'You were right. This will just be another point in favour of her family. How is she supposed to take care of herself with her present injuries?'

'I'm working on it.'

'I'm sure you are,' she replied with admiration.

The door to the tearoom opened and Alex walked in. 'Hi. I was told the two of you were in here.' He was dressed in theatre scrubs and sat down next to Sally.

'Busy night?' she asked.

'It's just beginning to start. Almost eleven-thirty, and already I've had two emergencies.'

'Sounds to me,' Jed said, not looking up from what he was writing in Mrs Marks's notes, 'as though you need some help.'

'That's right,' Sally picked up Jed's cue. 'Have you thoroughly read through Jordanne's résumé?'

'Yes, I have.'

'Well?' Sally pressed.

'She's good—on paper, that is.'

'Excuse me?' Jed frowned with indignation and this time stopped writing. When he saw that Alex was smiling, he shook his finger at him. 'Don't go making jokes about my little sister. I'm very protective of her and just for the record, mate, she's a brilliant orthopaedic surgeon, isn't she, Sally?'

'No doubt about that,' Sally replied immediately.

'I knew you two would take her side,' Alex teased.

'It's not about taking sides,' Jed persevered. 'It's about finding a solution to your overworked schedule. Jordanne set me up with Sally and—' He stopped, realising how that might sound. 'Professionally speaking, of course,' he continued.

'Of course,' Alex agreed readily, trying to hide a smile.

'And Sally has been an immense asset…to my clinic.' As he said the words his gaze encompassed Sally who was surprised at the praise.

She smiled at him, feeling a little self-conscious. 'Thank you.'

'I speak the truth.' He broke the gaze and glanced quickly

at Alex, before returning his attention to Mrs Marks's case notes.

Sally watched him for a few seconds then turned to Alex. 'So, what's the verdict? Does Jordanne get the job?'

'In actual fact, that's the reason I sought the two of you out. I received a letter this morning from one of the avenues I pursued for funding—a pharmaceutical company which is willing to sponsor a twelve-month orthopaedic research fellowship. It means that the research I've been wanting to do out at the Institute can now be started and...' He paused and looked at them both. 'It also means that Jordanne has a job.'

'Have you told her?' Jed asked as he closed the case notes and stood.

'Yes. I called her earlier this evening. She'll begin work once I get back from the conference in a few weeks' time.'

'Excellent,' Sally said, and smiled at Alex. 'You've made a wise decision, Alex.'

'I agree with Sally.' Jed walked over and shook his friend's hand. 'You won't regret it.'

'That's still to be seen,' Alex said solemnly. ''When I spoke to Jordanne and told her the news, she screamed in my ear, dropped the phone and laughed for a full minute.' Alex frowned.

'That's Jordanne!' Sally and Jed said in unison. They smiled at each other, their gazes holding for a moment before Jed turned away.

'I need to go and check on Mrs Marks.' With that, he walked out of the room.

Sally watched him go, yearning for him to return the instant he disappeared from her sight. She had it bad, she reasoned. A bad case of Jed-itis. She returned her attention to Alex who was still frowning. 'Don't worry about Jordanne's exuberance. You'll get used to it.'

'I don't know.' He shook his head slowly. 'I have the distinct feeling that I may have made a huge mistake.'

'Don't be silly, Alex,' Sally chided. 'Jordanne is a very competent orthopaedic surgeon.'

'Have you worked with her before?'

'Yes. Several times.'

'And? Be honest, now.'

'I'm always honest. As I've said, Jordanne's a good surgeon. She's good with the patients, she's good with administration.' Sally shrugged. 'She's good at everything.'

'But not brilliant,' he pointed out.

'Alex,' she cajoled and stood up. 'You've made the right decision. Jordanne is the perfect person to lighten your load and help with your research. I'd better check on Mrs Marks, too.' She walked towards the door.

'Hey—how are things going with Jed?'

It was Sally's turn to frown. 'I wish I knew. One minute he's hot and the next he's cold.'

'Hot is good and cold is bad?'

'Yes. He also seems awfully concerned about you. Care to shed some light on that?'

Alex smiled. 'I thought I told you to figure it out.'

'I did, but it only resulted in Jed being jealous of you. What's there to be jealous about? There's nothing going on between us.'

'You know that and I know that...' Alex wiggled his eyebrows up and down as he followed Sally to the door.

'What have you said to him?'

'Nothing,' he denied. 'Actions speak louder than words.'

'Alex?' she asked, her tone holding a warning.

'Hey.' He held up his hands defensively. 'I'm just trying to help two good friends come to their senses.' He walked past her and into the corridor.

'What?' She went after him. 'What does that mean?'

He stopped, turned and gave her a look of amazement. 'Sally, if you don't know, I'm certainly not going to tell you.' He paused and when she didn't say anything he continued, 'I'm due back in Theatre. I'll try and catch up with you before I go to the conference—otherwise, I'll see you when I return.'

'Sure.' She nodded absent-mindedly and walked in the opposite direction towards Recovery. As the doors swished open to admit her, she quickly scanned the room for Jed. There he was, standing next to Mrs Marks's bed, reading the observation notes.

Sally's palms became clammy and beads of perspiration formed on her forehead. It wasn't overly hot in here but as her heart hammered wildly beneath her ribs one fact was clear, and it was definitely designed to raise her blood pressure.

She was in love with Jed McElroy!

CHAPTER SEVEN

'WHEN Mum decides to throw you a birthday party, she really throws a party,' Joel told his brother as they stood to the side of the large family room which had been turned into a dance floor.

'That's Mum.' Jed shrugged and took a sip from his wine-glass. Once more his gaze scanned the room for Sally. She was wearing the most stunning black dress that hugged every delicious curve of her body, except for her shoulders which were bare. Finally his gaze settled on her and he exhaled slowly. She was talking to Jordanne.

'What do you think?' Joel was asking.

'Sorry. Say that again—I wasn't listening.' Jed's gaze didn't waver from Sally and Joel followed the object of his brother's attention.

'She's nice.'

'Hmm?' This time Jed looked quickly at his brother, a frown on his face.

'Sally. She's nice.'

'Oh, yeah. She is.'

'So…what's going on between the two of you?' Joel's question was accompanied by eyebrows that he wiggled up and down in a suggestive manner.

'Nothing,' Jed growled.

Joel laughed. 'I tend to disagree with you there, big brother.'

'What's that supposed to mean?'

'Well, when I held the gorgeous Sally in my arms while we danced earlier, all *she* could talk about was you and all *you* could do was glare daggers at me.'

'That's absurd,' Jed protested.

'Is it?' As they watched, Jared, the youngest of Jed's siblings, interrupted Sally's and Jordanne's conversation, and although they couldn't hear what he was saying, moments later Sally and he were dancing alongside other guests.

'See?' Joel pointed out. 'You've clenched not only your teeth but your hand as well. Jared's a happily married man *and* your brother. Why should it bother you so much that he's dancing with your employee?'

Sally laughed at something Jared had said and Jed turned away, unable to watch. The way her neck curved up, the exposure of her creamy, satin skin. It was all too much for him.

'If it pains you so much to see her dancing with other men, brothers or not, then go and do something about it.'

Jed concentrated on unclenching his hands and forced himself to relax. 'You know something, bro? You might just have a point.' Jed thrust his almost full glass of wine at Joel, before casually making his way towards Sally.

He tapped Jared on the shoulder. 'May I cut in?'

'Sure,' Jared said amicably. 'Nice to talk to you, Sally. Come over and meet my wife later.'

'Thanks, Jared.' Sally settled her hand into Jed's as the classical band changed tempo and played a slow waltz. The warmth of his arm as it encircled her waist sent shivers up and down her spine.

'I feel as though I've hardly seen you this past week,' he began, and Sally had a hard time raising her gaze to meet his.

'It *was* rather busy,' she agreed. She swallowed, trying to get rid of the dryness in her throat.

'Did Alex get away all right for the conference?'

'I'm not sure.' All Sally was sure of was the frantic pounding of her heart. Ever since she'd realised she was in love with Jed, she'd been filled with such a mixture of emotions that she was having a hard time keeping them all straight.

'You didn't see him before he left?'

'No.' She was so conscious of the way her hand felt in his, her other hand resting lightly on his shoulder. It brought back the memory of that incredible kiss they'd shared just over a week ago with force. She didn't want to talk about Alex—she wanted to concentrate on being with him.

She'd answered him only with monosyllables on Friday night after she'd recognised her true feelings. All weekend she'd stayed at home, willing the phone to ring and for Jed to casually ask her out, but it didn't ring. On Monday she'd done her best to avoid him, and by Wednesday she'd begun to realise that the avoidance game they were playing was mutual. On Thursday evening, Jed had driven to Sydney in order to help his parents with the party preparations.

Sally had flown the short distance from Canberra to Sydney and taken a taxi from the airport to Jordanne's apartment where she was due to sleep the night, before returning to Canberra early tomorrow morning ready for work again on Monday.

They danced on for a while, both content to simply be in each other's company. Sally willed Jed to draw her closer, to feel the warmth of his body against hers once more, but he continued to hold her at a respectable distance.

'Where are you staying tonight?'

'At Jordanne's.'

'Oh?' He seemed surprised.

'Something wrong?'

He shook his head. 'I thought you might have stayed at your parents' home.'

'As far as I know, they don't even know I'm here—in Sydney, I mean.'

'And that's the way you'd like it to stay.' He smiled down at her. 'From what you've told me, I can understand that.'

Sally returned his smile and gave his hand a little squeeze. 'Thanks.'

The smile disappeared from Jed's face and he cleared his throat. 'We need to talk.' He glanced at the people surrounding them. 'But not here. Come with me.'

Jed continued to hold her hand while he safely navigated them through the maze of people.

'Jed!' A big burly man called, and headed in Jed's direction.

'Oh, no.'

'Problem?'

'Anatomy professor from med school. Talks for hours. Meet me in the library. I'll try to be as quick as I can. Go.'

Sally turned and walked away. She felt far from calm as she thought of her secret rendezvous with Jed but hoped she looked as though she were enjoying herself. Her internal excitement began to mount to an uncontrollable level. Jed wanted to talk with her—privately. That could only mean one thing—couldn't it? Now, if she could only find the library.

'Sally,' Jane McElroy said as they nearly bumped into each other around a corner, 'I'm so glad you could make it. I've been looking forward to meeting you.'

Jed's parents had been circulating furiously at the beginning of the party, making sure all the guests were welcomed into their home. Now that the party was in full swing, Jane was obviously relaxing a little.

'Jordanne has told me so much about you over the years, I feel as though we're good friends.'

'I feel the same.' Sally smiled warmly.

Jane took Sally's hand in hers and patted it. 'Promise me you'll come and stay with us one weekend when my tyrant of a son isn't working you too hard. It would be great to catch up without so many people around.'

'That sounds…' The words stuck in her throat and tears began to well in her eyes. 'That sounds lovely.' Jane radiated the nurturing motherly love Sally had lived without for her entire life. To be invited to come and spend a weekend with them, to be accepted into their home, no questions asked, was almost a dream come true.

'Oh, darling.' Jane placed her arm around Sally's shoulders. 'Jordanne's told me about your parents, in the strictest confidence, of course, and I empathise with your situation. I'm an only child.'

'You are?'

'Why do you think I had so many children?' Jane laughed. 'The invitation is genuine. Any time you feel the need to escape, feel free to come here.' Jane tenderly wiped the tears from Sally's eyes with a tissue. 'Don't want to ruin your make-up, dear, and you look so lovely tonight.'

'Thank you.'

'It's no wonder my son can't keep his eyes off you.'

Sally's eyes widened in surprise. 'Um…' She hesitated, but Jane only laughed.

'He's been my son for forty-two years. I know him very well. I'd better check on the food. I'm glad John talked me into hiring caterers but I still like to feel in control.' Jane gave Sally's shoulder a squeeze before leaving her alone.

Sally sighed and continued down a corridor. It was a large house but she figured, with eight people having lived under one roof, it had to be.

She opened a door and discovered a bathroom. She shut the door and opened another one further down the corridor. A sewing room.

'Two more doors down on the right,' a deep voice she'd recognise anywhere said from behind her. 'I thought you'd have been there by now.'

She turned and smiled up at him as he fell into step beside her. 'You weren't the only one who got waylaid,' she offered by way of explanation.

'I know. I saw you talking to my mother.'

'She's such a lovely person, Jed. I envy you.'

He opened a door and switched on the light, waiting for her to precede him. 'I can see why you would, but many people would envy you, too.' He closed the door behind him. 'Being able to have anything and everything you've ever wanted. Having servants to do your bidding.'

'Never seeing your father, hardly ever seeing your mother and basically having no real friends my own age,' Sally finished for him. She turned and faced him. 'All I wanted was someone to love me. *Really* love me for who I am deep down inside, but…for so long I had no idea who I was.'

'Did the Olympics help you find out?'

'Yes, which is why, I guess, I'm more concerned about

Alice than I should be. If she can learn from my life…' Sally
trailed off and rubbed her hands on her bare arms as a chill
swept over her. Jed must have seen the action because he
quickly took off his jacket and crossed to drape it around her
shoulders.

'Oh, thank you,' she replied, and looked up at him. She
smiled, feeling rather shy all of a sudden. 'I guess my dress
isn't quite…suitable for winter.'

'No. It's not,' he admitted gruffly, and turned away from
her. Both of them remained silent and Sally wasn't sure what
to do. Jed had been the one to suggest they talk more privately.
She looked at his back, his crisp white shirt ironed to perfection, the way his trousers gently outlined his long legs.

'We need to talk,' he said, and turned around, catching her
staring at him. Sally quickly looked at the floor and pulled his
jacket more tightly around her shoulders. Slowly she met his
gaze only to find that he was frowning.

'Yes.' She nodded once, agreeing with him.

Jed put his hands into his pockets and took a step closer.
He took his hands out again and came closer still. He stopped
just in front of her and looked down into her upturned face.

'I want to apologise for kissing you last week. I was caught
up in the heat of the moment and I want you to know it won't
happen again.'

Sally was puzzled. This was the last thing she'd expected
him to say. She opened her mouth to say something but he
held up a hand.

'No, please, don't say anything just yet. Let me finish.' He
cleared his throat and continued. 'I know you and Alex have
hit it off from the start and I don't want to intrude in your
relationship. I guess if he wasn't such a good friend and you
weren't my employee then things might be a bit easier.' Jed
raked a hand through his hair and walked away from her as
though the distance might help him to think straight. 'But I
also want to caution you.'

So Alex *had* been right. Jed *did* think they were a couple.
His attitude over the past few weeks slowly began to make

sense. Sally tried to hide her smile. Jed was being terribly serious. 'Caution me?'

'Yes. Please, don't take this the wrong way. I...enjoyed our kiss—far too much, in fact—but you responded so ardently to my touch.' He shook his head as though trying to clear the mental image away. 'Alex is a good mate. Don't mess him around. Don't go kissing other men if you have serious feelings for Alex. It's not fair. Not to you and certainly not to him.'

If anyone else had spoken to her like this, Sally would have been livid, but the man she loved was being so respectable and so darn cute that she was having a hard time holding onto her laughter.

'I've offended you,' he continued when she didn't reply.

'No,' she said quickly. 'You haven't. I was just thinking about what you've said. You're a good friend to Alex, Jed.' Sally took a step towards him, then another, and then another, closing the distance that separated them, her gaze never once leaving his. Jed remained where he was and she saw his eyes widen in surprise at her attitude. His Adam's apple worked overtime as he swallowed.

'But you've got the wrong end of the stick.'

'Hmm?' Jed pulled at his shirt collar with his finger. 'What?'

Sally raised her hands and slowly loosened his tie. Next she undid the top button of his shirt, then the next button and then the next. She pushed the shirt open whilst caressing his chest lightly with her fingertips. She shivered with delight as their flesh made contact. *Never* in her life had she behaved as wantonly as she was doing now. Then again, she'd *never* been in love before.

Jed's hands came up and encircled her wrists. 'I don't think...you understand what I just said.' He swallowed again.

'Jed. I understand perfectly.' Her wrists might have been captive but her lips were free. She dipped her head forward and placed a kiss on his chest. The shudder that ripped through him filled her with a stronger sense of confidence. Just knowing that she could make him feel this way, that she had power over his emotions, it decreased the vulnerability she'd felt when she'd first realised she was in love with him.

'Sally,' he groaned, his eyes closing as he fought for composure. His grip on her wrists relaxed and she eased one of her hands free. 'We can't.'

'Yes, we can,' she disagreed.

'He's a good friend. I can't betray him—his trust—like th—'

'Shh.' She placed a finger onto his lips. 'Alex means nothing to me, Jed,' she whispered as she pressed her lips once more to the warmth of his chest.

'He does,' Jed contradicted. 'I've seen the way you look at him.'

Sally eased her head back and gazed up at the man she knew was her soul mate. 'Look at me, Jed.' She waited for him to open his eyes and gaze down into hers. 'Do I look at Alex the way I'm looking at you now?' She shook her head, answering her own question. 'We're friends—*nothing more.*'

'I want to believe it,' he uttered as his head lowered towards her own.

'Then believe it,' she urged, waiting impatiently for his lips to be on hers. His breath fanned across her face and Sally's eyelids fluttered closed.

'Sally, I don't—'

Her impatience won out as she freed her other wrist, clamped her hands on either side of his head and forced it downwards. When their lips met, both of them relaxed into the embrace—Jed wrapping his arms protectively around Sally's body, Sally lacing her fingers through his hair.

Fireworks burst continuously throughout her body as the sparks from Jed's kiss ignited every fibre within her. His mouth was hot and hungry on hers and she matched his intensity without thought. It was completely different from their first kiss which had been more exploratory, more searching.

Jed's arms slightly loosened their grip as he eased back

from her. Sally tightened her grip on his head, never wanting to let him go.

This was where she belonged—the place she'd been searching for throughout the past thirty-four years. It was here, in Jed's arms. In Jed's life. Hopefully, in Jed's heart.

He tore his lips from hers but only to blaze a trail of tiny and erotic kisses down her neck. He shoved his jacket impatiently from her shoulders and kissed the skin revealed. His kisses traced the line of her dress across the front of her chest and it was Sally's turn to shudder with uncontrollable delight.

'You taste so…incredible… Good enough to eat,' he murmured as he slowly worked his way back up her neck towards her lips. 'Do you have any idea how long I've been waiting to hold you in my arms and kiss you this way?'

'Tell me,' she whispered.

He looked down into her eyes and she knew the burning passion he saw there was the same she saw in his. 'From the moment I opened your car door after watching your Mercedes swerve all over the road in such a horrifying manner.'

'I think you should have,' she responded with a small smile. 'Why?'

'Because that's all I wanted you to do. My knight in shining armour.' Sally pushed a lock of hair back from his face.

Jed's mouth covered hers again and Sally sighed with happiness. A few minutes later they sprang apart guiltily at the knock on the library door.

'Jed?' his mother called. 'It's time for the cake. Come and blow out your candles—if you have any breath left,' she added with a chuckle.

Sally and Jed looked at each other before they both burst out laughing.

'Caught like a couple of teenagers,' Jed said, and Sally nodded.

'You might want to comb your hair,' she suggested as she raked her fingers through her own. 'It looks as though you've just got out of bed.'

They stared at each other at the mention of the word 'bed'.

Jed's gaze was still smouldering with desire and Sally knew they both had to be strong. He had a roomful of guests waiting for him.

Jed picked up his jacket from where it had landed carelessly on the floor. He took her hand in his. 'Come on.'

Sally pulled her hand away and he looked at her quizzically. 'Something wrong?'

'I…well, I don't know if I'm ready for everyone to know…you know…that we're…' She trailed off and looked down at the ground for a moment.

'That we're a couple?' he asked, and Sally raised her gaze to meet his.

'Yes.'

'*Are* we a couple?' His tone was soft and he brushed his fingers tenderly over her cheek.

Sally smiled at him. 'I'd like us to be.'

'Me, too.' The smile was reciprocated and Jed placed a quick kiss on her lips before turning to open the door. 'After you, Dr Bransford.'

'Thank you.' Sally was *very* conscious of Jed being directly behind her as they exited from the library. There was no one in the corridor and for that she was grateful. 'I think I'll go freshen up a bit,' she told him, and he winked at her, making her feel all tingly and mushy again.

In the bathroom, Sally took some long deep breaths and eyed her reflection critically. Her eyes were still glazed with passion and her lips were swollen as though she'd just been thoroughly kissed—which she had! This, however, wasn't what she wanted everyone else at the party to realise.

After brushing her hair and repairing her make-up, she checked her dress. 'Perfect,' she announced to the mirror.

When she returned to the party, Jed was standing with his parents and siblings surrounding him, a large rectangular cake in front with a blaze of candles. Jordanne, Joel and Justin with their father John were on one side of Jed, whilst Jasmine and Jared with their mother were on the other.

Jed's gaze locked with Sally's across the crowded room and

he smiled warmly at her. She watched as he whispered something to his father, and from where she stood it looked as though he'd said, 'Now we can begin.' Sally realised he'd been waiting for her! The knowledge warmed her heart but made her feel very self-conscious at the same time.

She looked across at Jordanne who was also looking at Sally in amazement. Sally simply smiled back before turning her attention to Jed's father who was about to make a speech.

John McElroy, as head of the clan, kept it short and soon they were all invited to sing 'Happy Birthday' to Jed. When it came time for Jed to blow out the forty-two candles, he almost did it in one breath but not quite. Another attempt was required and this prompted Jared to tease him.

'You needed to take one breath, big brother,' Jared said with a laugh. 'That means you have one girlfriend.' It was obviously a game they'd played during childhood as the other siblings laughed—all except Jordanne, who was still eyeing Sally carefully.

Jed smiled at his youngest brother but didn't comment. He thanked all his guests once more for coming before requesting the band to begin playing again.

Almost the instant the music began Sally felt a hand on her arm. She turned around to see Jordanne, a curious expression on her face.

'Can we talk?'

'Ah…sure.' It seemed to be a night for talking, Sally thought to herself. Jordanne led her into a corner where there weren't too many people.

'What's going on between you and Jed?' she asked quietly.

'You were never one to beat about the bush, Jordanne.' Sally sighed and looked at her watch. 'As of a whole fifteen minutes ago your brother and I are now officially…dating, I think would be the word for it.'

'*Really?*' Jordanne's eyes were wide with astonishment. 'When? You've never said *anything* about him.'

Sally shrugged. 'I felt…uncomfortable talking to you about your own brother.'

'So Kirsten knows?'

'Yes. Well, she knows I have feelings for Jed but, then, *he* knows that now.' Sally searched the room for him and found him playing with one of his nieces. Her heart warmed at the sight. She returned her attention to Jordanne. 'I know you're probably feeling a little left out but, truly, I didn't mean to hurt you. I just didn't want you to get your hopes up in case nothing happened and, well, I guess I was also a bit concerned in case you didn't approve of me for him.'

'How could I not?' Jordanne said, a smile beginning to light her face. 'I couldn't have matched you two better if I'd tried myself. Why do you think I initially thought of Jed for your Ph.D. supervisor? I thought you two would have a lot in common.'

'You're not angry?' Sally asked hopefully.

'No—a little depressed that you felt you couldn't confide in me but I can see your point of view.'

'Please, don't say anything just yet,' Sally asked.

'Problem?'

Sally shook her head. 'I need time to…adjust, I guess the word is, to it being, well, official.' She laughed. 'I know that probably sounds silly but—'

'No, it doesn't. I know you, remember. I know you need time to process new experiences but, please, tell me one thing and be totally honest here. How do you *really* feel about Jed?'

'Talk about being put on the spot,' Sally jested, hoping to find a way around this question.

'Sally,' Jordanne said seriously.

Sally sighed again and looked Jordanne squarely in the eyes. 'You must promise not to breathe a word to Jed. We've only just begun—'

'Yes, yes, all right,' Jordanne replied impatiently.

Here was the moment of truth—the first time she'd admitted her feelings to anyone else. Her throat was suddenly dry and she swallowed. 'I'm in love with him.'

'*Yes!*' came Jordanne's reply, and she hugged her friend tightly.

'Jordanne? I need air.' Sally said after a moment.

'Sorry. I'm so happy for both you and Jed.'

'Thanks, but remember…'

'Not a word,' Jordanne promised, and crossed her heart.

'What is she promising now?' Jed asked as he came to stand beside Sally—*close* beside Sally. She could feel the warmth of his body, smell the heady scent of his cologne and feel the gentle touch of his fingers with hers.

Sally tentatively raised her gaze to meet his and when he smiled down at her her knees threatened to give way but she ordered them to stand firm.

Jordanne reached up and kissed her brother on the cheek.

'What's that for?' he asked, and looked from his sister to Sally. 'Ah, I see. You two have been talking.' He nodded and grazed his fingers lightly across Sally's lower back, leaning down to say softly, 'I thought you said you didn't want to make it public knowledge?'

Sally's breathing increased at his touch and her stomach flipped over several times. 'Well… I um…'

Jed laughed, a rich deep sound that filled Sally with pleasure. 'I'm only teasing,' he said. 'Jordanne's a master at wheedling bits of information from people.'

'You taught me everything I know, big brother,' Jordanne quipped, and looked up. 'Shh. Here comes Joel.'

Sally felt Jed's hand drop back to his side and instantly felt bereft.

'So,' Joel said as he joined their little circle, 'I see you've taken my advice, Jed.'

'Exactly which bit of wisdom are you referring to?' Jed asked with a large grin.

Joel only nodded. 'If you don't know, then I'm not going to tell you. There is, however, one way to put it to the test.' Joel looked at Sally. 'Would you care to dance with me again?'

Sally smiled warmly at Joel. 'I'd be delighted,' she said, without even looking at Jed for confirmation.

'Excellent,' Joel said, and offered his arm to Sally.

'Maintain a respectable distance,' Jed told his brother politely, 'or I'll be breaking both your arms.'

'Yep. You took my advice,' Joel replied smugly as he led Sally onto the dance floor.

'Are you going to tell me what the advice was?' Sally asked.

'I told him to do something about the way he was feeling, and *now* look at him,' Joel replied. 'He's nowhere near as tense as he was the last time I danced with you.'

'Is there *any* way of keeping secrets in this family?'

'Absolutely none. We're all very close and that means we can read each other like a book.'

'So…Jared, Jasmine and Justin?'

'And Dad, too,' Joel added. 'We all knew the instant Jed waited for you to be in the room before he allowed Dad's speech to proceed.'

'I see.'

'So, should I say welcome to the family?'

'Not just yet,' Sally advised, and then in an attempt to change the subject she asked, 'From what I can remember of your family, you're the GP—is that correct?'

'Oh, Jed's *definitely* done something about it,' he crowed.

'Please, explain.'

'Earlier, when we danced, all you could talk about was him. *Now* you're willing to find out about me.'

Sally nodded. 'Well, are you going to tell me?'

'Yes.' Joel smiled at her. There was a strong family resemblance between the siblings—all had dark brown hair and their father's blue eyes. Jasmine, though, had coloured her hair blonde and stood out from the rest of the McElroys. When Joel smiled at Sally, though, there were no lightning bolts as when his oldest brother smiled in almost an identical way.

'You are correct, I'm the GP. Jordanne is the only other member of the family to go into medicine. Justin and Jared run a computer business and have just gone into partnership with Jasmine's husband, Edward. Very incestuous,' he added.

'And Jasmine loves to decorate.'

Joel raised his eyebrows. 'Been to Jed's house, have you?'

'Jordanne tells me that you like to ski?'

Joel laughed, knowing she was changing the subject again, and this time he let her. 'Like? No. *Love* to ski is a better description. When I'm on that hill with brilliant white snow all around me I feel so tranquil, so relaxed. Jordanne's also probably told you that I've locumed for the last few years in order to train overseas.'

Sally nodded.

'I'm hoping to make the team for the next Winter Olympics.'

Sally frowned. 'Haven't you already competed in several Olympics? I thought Jordanne had said you'd won a silver medal in the cross country.'

'That's right but as my age is now against me, I thought I'd give it one last try. See if I can go for the gold.'

'If not?'

'Then I'm extremely happy with my silver.'

'Good for you,' Sally encouraged. 'It's…an incredible experience.'

'Skiing?' Joel asked, a little puzzled.

'No, the Olympics.' Sally told Joel briefly about her medal, astonishing him completely.

'Jordanne never said anything.'

'I asked her not to,' Sally explained.

'Wow. I'm dancing with a gold medallist.' Joel straightened his shoulders with pride.

'And I'm dancing with a silver medallist. So when do you "hit the slopes" next?'

'Tomorrow. I broke my training regime for Jed's party but that's it for the rest of the season. The snow so far has been excellent considering it's almost the end of July.'

'That's enough,' Jed said as he came up behind Joel. 'I want her back now.'

'You've been very restrained, big brother. I'm proud of you. Thank you for sharing your gold medallist with me.' With that Joel stepped aside to allow Jed to dance with Sally.

Jed placed his arm about Sally's waist, and where he'd pre-viously held her at a respectable distance, this time he edged quite a bit closer. 'Are you used to the idea of *us* yet?'

She looked up into his face and smiled. 'I hope I *never* get used to the way you make my knees go weak just by smiling at me. Or the way my body melts every time you touch me. I can't help the fact that your family is so close knit that they know what's going on before either of us, but to answer your question, I'm more accustomed to *us* than I was half an hour ago.'

Jed's gaze smouldered with desire at her words. 'Good,' he said, and bent his head to claim her lips in a brief but sensual kiss. Right in front of everyone!

CHAPTER EIGHT

ON SUNDAY morning, Sally had cancelled her flight back to Canberra in order to drive with Jed the short three-hour trip back to the ACT. Jed had picked her up from Jordanne's and together they'd had a wonderful time.

'I'm glad you decided to come back with me.'

'We're a couple now. Well and truly after that kiss you gave me last night.'

Jed laughed and Sally delighted at the sound.

'It's just as well there were no reporters around, although somehow, some way, I *know* what happened will get back to my father. Someone always knows someone else and so on.'

'Is that a bad thing?' Jed asked cautiously.

'What? My father knowing about us? Not…really.'

'Meaning?'

'Well, he hasn't given you his stamp of approval, has he? My father likes to be in control and considering *he* hasn't chosen you…' Sally trailed off. She watched as Jed clenched his jaw and knew he was remembering his previous encounter with Anya's father.

Sally placed a hand on Jed's thigh, still marvelling that she had the right to touch him. 'Regardless of his opinion, it makes no difference to how I feel.'

She could tell he was trying to relax. 'And how do you feel…about me, I mean?'

Sally went to withdraw her hand from his thigh but he wouldn't let her, holding her hand captive beneath his. Was it too soon to tell him she loved him? They were almost at the end of their journey and he'd turned the car in the direction of her town house.

When she didn't say anything, Jed asked, 'Too soon?'

'It's not that,' she replied quickly.

'Then what?'

'We're almost at my place. Come on in and we can discuss things.'

'Uh-oh. That sounds ominous.'

'It wasn't meant to be.'

They were both silent until Jed stopped the car outside Sally's town house and cut the engine. She clambered out and waited for Jed to retrieve her overnight bag from the boot of his car.

'I'll carry it. You get the door.'

Sally did as he'd suggested, and once they were both inside she quickly switched on the heating. 'Tea?'

'Yes, thanks.'

She'd half expected him to stay in the lounge room as he'd done on previous occasions and was therefore surprised when he followed her into the kitchen. He watched as she switched on the kettle and prepared everything. Sally leaned back against the bench to wait for the water to boil. Jed took the few steps that separated them and stood in front of her.

Leaning forward, he placed a hand on either side of her, their faces close. He brought his lips into contact with hers and Sally relaxed with a sigh. It had been almost an hour since he'd last kissed her and she was beginning to have withdrawal symptoms.

'Sally Elizabeth Bransford...' he whispered when he pulled away. 'I'm one hundred per cent certain that I'm in love with you.' He claimed her lips once more and crushed his body up against hers.

Sally wound her arms around his neck and kissed him back with fervent passion, her heart and soul exploding with love for this man.

Breathlessly, he eventually allowed her to push him away. 'Really, Jed?' she asked. 'Do you really love me?' Her gaze searched his, desperate for the answer.

'Yes,' he replied instantly, and she saw it reciprocated in his eyes.

She smiled shakily at him. 'It's what I've always longed for. Someone to love me *just* for me and not for any other reason.' The kettle boiled and switched itself off but Sally and Jed simply ignored it.

Sally took his face in both hands. 'You must know that I return your feelings, Jed, although I'm sorry to say I have no idea what your middle name is.'

He smiled at her. 'It's Thomas.'

'Jedidiah Thomas McElroy?'

'Yes.'

'Well, then, Jedidiah Thomas McElroy—I love you right back.' Sally stretched her neck and kissed him, sealing the mutual declaration of their love. When she tried to pull away, Jed deepened the kiss, evoking those overwhelming emotions she was becoming more familiar with.

Sally broke free and placed a finger on his lips. 'Wait here a moment.' She ducked under his arm and walked on unsteady legs out of the kitchen.

'What's wrong?' he asked.

'Nothing. Just make the tea for me, please, and sit down. I have to get something.'

'Don't be too long,' he called.

Sally raced into her bedroom where a large framed map of Botany Bay was leaning against her wall. Now was the most perfect time to give him his birthday present. She carried it carefully back to the lounge room where Jed was placing the teacups on the coffee-table.

'Happy birthday,' she said, and marvelled at the look of wonder on his face as he sank down into the lounge. Sally handed him the map.

'What? Where?' His eyes were large with amazement and he glanced from the map to her. 'Sally, I... It's incredible.'

'I'm glad you like it.' She came to sit beside him, leaning over his shoulder, her face close to his.

'*Like* it? Sally...' He gazed into her eyes before kissing her. 'You're amazing.'

'I know it said on your birthday invitation ''no presents

required'' but I couldn't resist this. Besides, I'd like to think I'm…well…different from everyone else who was at your party.'

'Special?' he asked, and she nodded. 'Sally, you are *very* special to me.' He kissed her again, long and slowly, before returning his attention to the map. 'The detail is remarkable. Where did you find it?'

'In a box in my garage.'

'*What?*'

Sally smiled at him. 'When my paternal grandfather passed away I…inherited, I suppose you'd call it, a lot of his personal effects. I went through them at the time, which wasn't long after I'd finished med school. It wasn't until I saw those maps in your study that I remembered seeing one rolled up in a cardboard tube in the box of his things. I checked it out and had it framed.'

Jed looked at her for a long moment. 'I love you,' he said softly, and kissed her lightly before motioning to the map. 'Thank you. I will cherish this for ever simply because you gave it to me.'

'I'm glad.' Sally was overwhelmed with his response. She'd never given anyone anything they would cherish. She smiled at him, tears starting to well in her eyes at the emotional moment. She kissed him again, pressing her lips firmly against his before deepening the kiss, showing him exactly how much she loved him.

The phone rang and they reluctantly pulled apart. 'You'd better get that,' he prompted, and stood up, carrying his map over to the wall. 'Do you mind if I take a look at it up on a wall?'

Sally shook her head as she leaned across the lounge and reached for the receiver. She cleared her throat before saying, 'Dr Bransford.' Jed removed one of her classic prints from the wall.

'Sally. It's Alex.'

'Hi, Alex.' She watched as Jed turned to look at her, wariness in his eyes. 'What can I do for you?' Her gaze never left Jed as he slowly returned to his task of hanging the map on the wall.

'I've been trying to contact Jed to wish him a happy birthday but I keep missing him. His mother suggested, and quite blasé she was about it, too, that I should try your place. So, is he there?'

Sally smiled. 'Yes.' She had to pull the phone away from her ear at his yell of delight. She laughed and returned the receiver to her ear. 'Would you like to speak to him?'

'You'd better believe it. Congratulations,' he added.

'Alex would like to speak with you.' Sally held the receiver out to Jed.

He took it and placed his hand over the mouthpiece. 'Why is he calling *you*?' Jed whispered.

'Jealous?' she teased, and laughed again. 'He's looking for you!'

With surprise, Jed raised the receiver to his ear.

'It's about time,' Alex blustered.

'What's that supposed to mean?'

'I've been doing everything I possibly could to help you realise you have feelings for that girl, and obviously it's worked.'

Jed was silent for a moment, digesting the information. 'I don't know whether to thank you or hit you,' he finally joked.

'The former will do fine. Promise me, though, that I can be best man at your wedding.'

'I don't see why not. I'll just check with Sally.'

Sally looked up at his words, her raised teacup to her lips. 'Alex wants to know if he can be best man at our wedding.'

It was the last thing she'd expected Jed to say and, unfortunately, she gulped on the hot tea and coughed, sending it spraying all over the coffee-table.

'I'll take that as a yes,' Jed replied. He didn't speak to Alex for much longer and was extremely jovial as he helped her clean up the mess she'd made.

'Wedding?' she asked.

'Moving a bit too fast for you?'

'Just a tad.'

'Right, then. Let's slow things down.'

And for the next fortnight, Jed and Sally took things slowly. Jed returned to his former routine of picking Sally up for work each morning and usually stayed for breakfast. In the evenings he'd cook them dinner at his house before taking her home. He didn't push her beyond that and Sally couldn't believe her good fortune.

Jed was everything she'd ever wanted in a man, and the fact that he was willing to concede to her wishes of taking things slowly she still found difficult to believe.

Alice Partridge was doing well with her rehabilitation but not as well as Sally would have liked. She had the feeling that Alice still had a lot of issues to sort through. Sally continued to visit her patient and thankfully had managed to avoid Gordon whenever he'd been in town.

Elena Marks was recovering well but her family had been continually harassing her. Her son had visited Jed and had once again asked for his mother to be declared not of sound mind. Jed had struggled to control his temper before asking Mr Marks to leave the premises.

He'd noted in Mrs Marks's chart that her sons weren't permitted to visit her any more as they were too disruptive and upsetting. If either of them attempted to contact their mother while she was in the hospital, he'd organise a restraining order on the grounds that it was affecting her recovery. The social worker on the ward agreed with Jed as together they were working towards a permanent solution on behalf of Mrs Marks. With all the legalities of the situation it would take them a while, but they were determined to succeed.

Two weeks after Jed's birthday party, both he and Sally were on call. It had been a quiet night so far and they'd enjoyed a leisurely dinner of lasagne and salad. Both were glad to be warm and cosy inside as the weather in the past few days had turned very wintry indeed. Sally gazed into the flickering flames of Jed's open fireplace as they snuggled on the lounge, the relaxing strains of Mozart filling the air.

'Glad to finally have your car back?' he asked.

'Most definitely,' Sally replied. 'It was an experience.'

'Just out of curiosity…' he cleared his throat and Sally felt him tense slightly '…why do you drive a Mercedes?'

'It was a graduation present.'

'From your father?'

'No. I wouldn't have accepted it from him. It was from my paternal grandfather. The car was his and he was so proud when I graduated from medical school that he gave it to me.'

'With personalised plates?'

'Yes. He was very ill and reasoned that he couldn't drive it anyway.' Sally sighed with remembrance and looked into the fireplace.

'Was he rich as well?'

Sally didn't miss the sneer in Jed's tone as he said the word 'rich'. 'Yes. My childhood memories of him were…not pleasant. He was a crotchety old man who only lived for his work. Yet when he became ill with emphysema, he changed. He must have realised his life was coming to an end. Six months before he died, I spent quite a bit of time with him. He said he was proud of me for standing up to my father. He also blamed himself for the way my father is—after all, he was only following in his own father's footsteps. It was a real…eye-opening time.'

'Did he and your father get along?'

'Not at all. They didn't even reconcile.'

They were both silent, caught up in thoughts and memories of their own. When the phone rang, Jed groaned. 'I knew it was too good to last.' He reached for the portable phone that he'd brought into the room, without disengaging himself from Sally.

'Dr McElroy.' He waited and whispered to Sally, 'It *is* the hospital.' He listened. 'What's the ETA?' Silence again. 'Right. See you soon.'

'I knew it was too good to last,' Sally said as the clock on the mantelpiece chimed eight.

As they made their way to the hospital in Jed's car, he filled her in on the sketchy details of the call.

'Accident at the snowfields. Two patients coming in. One is a young girl of thirteen so she'll go straight to Paediatrics. The other patient is an adult male. That's it.'

As neither of them were full time at the hospital, the gossip that had spread like wildfire regarding their relationship hadn't really affected them much. Now people were well and truly used to the idea so when they both walked into A and E, no one commented.

'Jed?' Triage Sister Renee Bourne called, and motioned for him to come across to her desk where she was speaking on the phone. Sally followed him.

'Good,' Renee said and noted something down. 'Thank you.' She replaced the receiver. 'That was Alex—he led the retrieval team. They'll be landing in about five minutes. They haven't been able to contact us due to terrible weather but, Jed…' She faltered and glanced at Sally, a worried expression on her face. 'It's your brother.'

Jed was silent for a moment as he processed the information.

Sally was shocked. 'Joel?'

'Yes.' Renee nodded for emphasis. 'Alex wanted you to know right away.'

'Show me the list of injuries,' he demanded, his jaw clenched tightly. Renee held the information out to him. 'Fractured right knee.' Jed shook his head. 'Poor Joel.'

Even Sally knew what anguish that would cause Jed's brother. Depending on how bad the damage was, Joel's odds of qualifying for the next Olympics were next to nothing.

'Fractured right tibia and fibula, fractured right first, second and third tarsals and metatarsals and fractured right patella— and that's just the *bones*.' Sally looked at Renee. 'What on earth happened?'

'We're not entirely sure. We received the list of injuries from the retrieval site but then interference from the snow and wind disconnected the call before we could get more information. That call…' she gestured to the phone '…was the only other time we've been contacted.'

'Let me know the instant they're here,' Jed said. 'I'll be in the tearoom.' With that he stalked off. Sally wasn't sure whether to follow him or not, but her intuition told her to leave him alone for the moment. She discussed a few more things with Renee before heading off. to Theatres to make sure everything was ready.

Sally and Theatre Sister Colleen Pomeray went over every possible scenario and what equipment they would need. It looked as though Sally was about to have her first operating experience with Alex as Jed wouldn't be permitted in Theatre. She changed out of her clothes into theatre attire and walked to the tearoom.

She paused outside the closed door, wondering whether she'd given Jed enough time. She knocked, unsure whether he wanted to be disturbed, and slowly opened the door.

'Where have you been?' he asked almost impatiently, and beckoned her in.

'Getting things ready in Theatre. I wanted to give you some privacy because I thought you'd be calling your parents.'

Jed crossed to her side and wrapped his arms around her. He placed a small kiss on her lips. 'I was. Thanks.'

'How are they?' Sally hugged him close, revelling in his warmth.

'Mum will be up worrying all night until she can speak to Joel herself. She'll call all the others and keep them informed.'

'How are *you* holding up?'

'When I see him I think I'll feel better. Not knowing exactly what happened, or what his injuries include, is the worst.'

'Total knee replacement?' Sally eased back and looked fentatively up at him.

'A high possibility and I sincerely hope for Joel's sake that it's not.' Jed broke free and started pacing the room, raking a hand through his hair in frustration. 'This was his final chance for a shot at the Olympics. He's no spring chicken.'

'He's only two years younger than you,' Sally reasoned, but

knew Jed had a point, especially where the Olympics were concerned. 'Besides, Olympic selection is based on performance, not age,' she added, trying to be optimistic. 'Joel has a wealth of experience and I'm sure he'll be up and back on the slopes in no time.'

'But if he has a total knee replacement, he'll be more likely to have further problems and in another five years or so will require a revision replacement. Regardless of what his knee is like today, this accident will also increase his risk of contracting osteoarthritis in the future. Once he has osteoarthritis—knee replacement. The cycle has begun. This will destroy him.'

'Joel has one thing that a lot of people don't have, and that's a family to support him and get him through the tough times.'

'Is it going to be enough?' Jed asked softly. 'Of one thing I'm certain—we all have a long time in Theatre ahead of us. Let's sit down and try to relax.'

He pulled out a chair for Sally as his pager beeped. 'That'll be Joel arriving,' he said, and checked the number.

They both hurried to A and E where a stretcher was being wheeled into trauma room one. The first thing Jed did was to grasp Alex's hand firmly in both of his.

'Thank you,' he murmured, before crossing to Joel's side.

'Joel?' Jed said, and waited for a response.

'Hey, big brother.' Joel slowly opened his eyes and gazed up at Jed. 'Hadn't planned on seeing *you* again so soon.'

Staff were all around them, taking vital signs and making sure that Joel was stabilised enough for Radiology.

'Sense of humour is still intact,' Jed muttered, and Sally saw him visibly relax. 'What happened?' Jed asked softly.

'Poor girl was going so fast she was out of control. It was almost dark and I only just saw her out of the corner of my eye as I was heading back in. I took off after her and managed to slow her down—to an extent—but both of us still crashed into a chairlift pylon.'

'Let me guess—you took the brunt of the collision.'

Joel closed his eyes. 'Yup,' he whispered. 'She would have—'

'Don't worry about it now,' Jed replied as he could see his brother starting to tense again. 'Ready for Radiology?' Jed asked Alex.

'Ready when you are.'

Jed stayed with his brother while Alex and Sally discussed the operations they'd be performing in more detail.

'The tibia will need an external fixator so that means the foot will need to be strapped once we've manipulated the fractures into alignment. The knee, though, we'll just have to wait and see.' Alex shook his head. 'How's Jed holding up?'

'Better now that's he's seen Joel. Although I think I should warn you that Jed's certain he'll be in Theatre with us.'

'I see.' Alex rubbed his thumb and index finger along his jaw. 'Ordinarily, I don't mind family members as spectators, but not in this instance. Do you agree?'

'Yes.'

'Then we need to be strong and hold firm on that, Sally.'

'Agreed.'

'Right. I think I'll go and get out of these bright orange overalls and into Theatre clothes. I'll meet you in Radiology.'

Sally went in search of Jed who, she discovered, was driving the radiographer insane with his possessive attitude.

'Tell me what's been going on,' she said, and pulled him away from Joel. Jed kept the lead apron on.

'They've just taken the last angle of the knee and are about to start on the tibia.'

'Good. Well…um…' Sally looked over Jed's shoulder at the radiographer, who was shooing them both away with her hands. 'Is Bethany on tonight?' Sally asked, and the radiographer nodded. 'Great. Why don't we go and see how's she's doing with the films?'

Jed looked at Joel.

'He's a big boy now,' Sally added as she helped Jed to take off the lead apron.

'Be back soon,' Jed told his brother. They went around to where they processed the films and found Bethany.

'Can't say I'm surprised to see you,' Bethany added when she saw them. 'How's Joel holding up?'

'He's fine. Analgesics are definitely working,' Jed responded.

'Good to hear. I'm doing the first film now,' she told them as she loaded it into the processing machine.

'At least you're not having to process them the old way again,' Sally commented with a smile.

'You know, sometimes I don't mind the old way,' Bethany said as the processing machine rattled. 'It's still not working properly.'

The instant Bethany took the film from the dryer she held it up so they could all see.

'Ouch!' Sally said in sympathy for Joel. The patella had been dislocated and at the top of the tibia there appeared to be a slight fracture of the lateral condyle.

'Looks positive,' Jed added as he took it from Bethany.

'Oh, no, you don't, Jed McElroy,' the radiographer chastised. 'Let me at least log it before you whisk it away.'

'You know me too well,' Jed reasoned with a sheepish grin. Sally laughed. Once more, Jed's relief was evident in his face. It looked as though Joel wouldn't require a total knee replacement. Surgery was paramount to get things back into place, but apart from that the long-term outlook was good.

'I'll go and find Alex,' he said, clutching the X-ray as though it were a lifeline.

'Thanks, Bethany,' Sally said with a smile. 'He was driving the radiographer up the wall.'

'You're welcome. So how are things going between the two of you?'

'Good,' Sally replied, feeling a little self-conscious. Of course, she had discussed things with Kirsten and Jordanne but they were her closest friends. Having other people asking her always made her feel slightly embarrassed. 'I'd better get going myself. I think Alex is going to need some back-up.'

'Why?' Bethany frowned.

'Because Jed thinks he's coming into Theatre with us.'

'Oh.' The single word was filled with a dawning realisation and Bethany nodded. 'Yes, I think you had better go. Jed's very protective when it comes to family—but, then, you'd know that.'

Sally didn't respond but took the next film which had been processed while they'd been talking and went in search of the men. It wasn't too difficult to find them once she'd entered Emergency Theatres. They were in the tearoom and both were being…quite loud.

'You have no right to restrict me,' Jed growled as Sally stood outside the door.

One of the theatre sisters caught her gaze and mouthed, 'Good luck,' to Sally as she rounded the corner into the room.

'And you're being unreasonable,' Alex countered.

They were facing each other, both obviously tense with the situation. It took a second or two for them to realise that Sally was in the room.

'Have you heard this?' Jed asked Sally as he crossed to her side and placed his arm around her waist. 'Alex won't allow me into Theatre to watch the operation. I'm not going to be doing anything, just watching.'

'You'll be leaning over my shoulder every step of the way, criticising everything I do,' Alex pointed out.

'Alex is right, Jed,' Sally said softly.

'What?' Jed dropped his arm instantly and looked at her as though she'd grown another head. 'You're *agreeing* with him?'

'He's the senior surgeon, Jed.' Sally reached out to him but he took a step away. That hurt but she pushed it aside. 'We both care about Joel, too, and you know we'll be using every skill we possess in fixing him up. Trust us.'

Jed turned his back on them. Sally glanced at Alex and shrugged. 'Alex thinks it's best if you stay out here, and I agree with him. I know you'll probably go stir crazy but that's the way it is, Jed.' No response. Sally continued, 'Right. Why don't we go to Theatre, Alex, and double check everything.'

Alex hesitated but Sally urged him out. She closed the door behind them. 'He just needs to come to terms with this decision. You know how he is—he likes to be in control of situations like this. We all do.'

Alex raked a hand through his hair. 'I feel as though I've really been pushing our friendship over the past month. First with getting him to realise his feelings for you and now this.' Alex spread his arms out wide before letting them drop dispiritedly to his sides.

'Why don't you check things out in Theatre and I'll speak to him by myself?'

'Good idea. You have ways of dealing with him that…well, I'd rather not employ.' Alex grinned cheekily.

Sally re-entered the tearoom to find Jed still standing in the same place, his back still to the door. She walked over and placed her arms about his waist—at least he didn't pull away.

Resting her head against his back, she listened to him breathe. 'I know this is difficult for you, Jed.'

He turned, enveloping her in the circle of his arms. 'I won't get in the way,' he pleaded like a little—lost—schoolboy. Sally's heart went out to him.

'Yes, you would and you know it. Do you trust Alex?'

'Yes.'

'And me?'

'Yes.'

'Then stop worrying. Joel will be fine. Now, why don't you give your parents a call and let them know that the knee isn't as bad as we initially thought?'

'Good idea,' he said flatly, and she knew he still wasn't happy about the situation but at least he was beginning to accept it. He called his parents and Sally returned to Radiology to see how things were progressing.

Joel had just had the last X-ray taken and she crossed to his side. 'Do you feel any pain?' she asked, and he opened his eyes from dozing.

'Hey, there. Pain? Oh, not much. The morphine's kicked in. Where's Jed?'

'Talking to your folks.'

'Mum must be worried out of her mind.'

'Jed's doing his best to alleviate that. I've come to check up on you and your X-rays.'

'Well, I can't speak for the X-rays, but I'm feeling real fine, missy.'

Sally laughed. 'Sounds as though the morphine is working well.'

Joel's smile disappeared. 'What's the news on my knee?'

'Better than we'd first anticipated. From the looks of things, you won't need a total knee replacement.'

Joel closed his eyes tightly for a second then opened them again. 'That's good news.'

'Good? It's fantastic. It means with rehab, you'll be back on those slopes you love so much before you know it.'

Joel looked up at her. 'Yes. You of all people understand what the true meaning of professional competition means.'

'It means a lot of work,' she said with a smile.

Bethany walked towards them, holding a large packet of X-rays. 'All done. How'd Jed take the news?'

'What news?' Joel asked.

'He wanted to be in Theatre when we operated and—'

'Alex said no,' Joel finished as he closed his eyes again, but this time he was much more relaxed. His hopes and dreams still had a chance of becoming a reality.

'Jed's fine,' Sally told Bethany and accepted the packet. 'Thanks. Right, let me find some orderlies to take you to Theatre prep and we'll be in business.'

The orderlies weren't too hard to track down and Sally once again thanked Bethany and the radiographer who'd taken the films, before heading back to the tearoom. Joel was seen by the anaesthetist whilst Jed, Alex and Sally poured over the films.

'Looks pretty straightforward,' Alex remarked. 'We'll tidy things up and put everything back into place.'

'I'll go have a quick word with Joel before he's anaesthetised,' Jed said, and together the three of them went to Theatres. Jed stayed with them while they scrubbed and gowned.

'Try and relax,' Sally offered with a smile just before they went in. 'We'll be out sooner than you know.'

Jed simply nodded and didn't smile back.

Sally and Alex entered Theatre and began the operation. They fixed the fracture at the centre of the tibia and fibula with plates and screws—the toes they would take care of at the end of the operation—but most of their time was taken up concentrating on the knee.

The phone shrilled to life when they were halfway through the operation. It was Jed, checking on their progress.

'The knee's not too bad,' Alex said out loud, and the scout nurse on the phone relayed the information to Jed. 'Anterior and posterior cruciate ligaments are badly damaged, partial tear to the lateral meniscus, popliteal tendon is strained—all the usual problems you'd find with a knee injury.'

It was as though there was an echo in the room as the scout nurse repeated Alex's information into the phone.

When Joel was wheeled to Recovery, Jed followed, although he was under strict orders from the sister in charge of Recovery to keep out of the way of her staff or she'd be asking him to leave.

Sally and Alex sat down in the tearoom for a much needed cuppa. The phone on the wall shrilled again. Sally and Alex looked at each other, both feeling fatigued.

'Throw?' Sally suggested, and Alex nodded. They both clenched their fists and shook them up and down three times before deciding between paper, scissors or rock. Sally chose paper—Alex chose scissors.

Admitting defeat, Sally crossed the room and answered the phone.

'Where are you?' It was Jordanne's voice on the other end of the line.

Sally frowned. 'Why? Where are you?'

'In A and E,' Jordanne announced.

'What? Um…hang on. I'll come and get you.' She replaced the receiver and looked at Alex. 'That was Jordanne. She's here.'

'Great,' he muttered. 'Another protective McElroy to deal with.'

Sally laughed. 'That's right. You two haven't met. Oh, you're going to just love Jordanne.' Feeling a renewed sense of energy at seeing her friend again, Sally had a spring in her step as she walked to A and E.

CHAPTER NINE

'JORDANNE!' Sally crossed to her friend who was standing by the A and E desk talking to a nurse. Dr Jordanne McElroy, M.B.B.S., F.R.A.C.S., was dressed in denim jeans and a large bright red knitted jumper with a huge coat over the top. Her long dark brown hair was all over the place, proof that the wind outside was rather strong.

Jordanne stopped in mid-sentence and took a few steps towards Sally. The two friends embraced.

'How is he?' Jordanne's blue eyes were searching for answers.

'He's doing just fine. Surgery went very well. Both Alex and I are thoroughly pleased.'

Jordanne reached down to collect her bags while Sally spoke. 'Great.'

'My goodness, how long are you staying for?' Sally took one of the large suitcases in her hands.

'I believe my contract is for twelve months.'

'You're starting *already*?' Sally couldn't believe the time had flown so quickly. They both said goodbye to the nurse and headed for Recovery. 'We can put your bags in the tearoom for now. I thought you weren't flying down until next weekend.'

'Why wait? Both Jed and Joel need me so when I heard about the accident I managed to change my flight to tonight.'

'Considering the weather, I'm surprised you weren't grounded.'

'We were for a few hours but then it cleared enough to fly. The ride was rather bumpy but I'm glad the airline decided to risk it.'

Sally walked through the open door of the tearoom. 'Oh.' She frowned.

'Something wrong?' Jordanne asked as she followed Sally in.

'Alex was in here. He must have gone to check on Joel.' They put Jordanne's bags and her coat against the wall, out of the way, and headed for Recovery.

Jed stood motionless beside his brother's bed, looking down at him while he slept. Sally and Jordanne walked quietly across. Jed wasn't surprised at seeing Jordanne, which meant he'd known she was coming. He placed a protective arm around his sister and together they both stood looking down at Joel.

Sally didn't know what to do. In one way she was envious of how supportive the McElroy family were of each other and in another way she felt completely left out. Jed must have read her thoughts because he looked up at that instant and held out his free hand to her.

Sally crossed to his side and Jed hugged her close. He kissed the top of Sally's head and breathed deeply. Jordanne eased out from beneath his arm and went around to the base of the bed to read Joel's chart. She nodded a few times, and when she looked up there was a glimmer of hope in her gaze.

'Thank you,' she said softly to Sally.

'I see the family reunion has begun,' Alex said from behind Jordanne. Sally watched as her friend spun around to look at him.

'I presume you're Alex?' Jordanne asked, still speaking in a whisper.

'That's right.'

Sally and Jed merely smiled as Jordanne flung her arms around Alex's neck and hugged him tight.

Alex held his arms out wide, his confused gaze meeting Jed's and Sally's over Jordanne's head.

'Thank you for rescuing my brother and operating on him.'

'Er…you're…um…welcome.'

Sally's gaze narrowed as she carefully observed Jordanne's

reaction to her new boss. Jordanne held Alex tightly for a few more moments before slowly releasing him.

Joel coughed and Alex took a step away from Jordanne.

'Joel? Everything all right?' Jed asked quietly.

As he spoke, Joel slowly opened his eyes. Both Jed and Jordanne were instantly at his side—one on each side of the bed.

'Everything OK?' Jed repeated.

'Mmm,' Joel murmured. A small smile twitched at his lips as he saw Jordanne. She bent to kiss her brother on the cheek.

'Howdy, stranger.'

'Hi.' He choked on the word and Jed quickly scooped up some ice chips and fed them to him.

'Better?'

'Mmm,' Joel answered. 'The girl?'

The two words were whispered but they all heard them.

'I knew you'd want to know,' Jed replied. 'I had one of the nurses ring through about fifteen minutes ago. The young girl you saved is out of Theatre and recovering well.'

Joel visibly relaxed and closed his eyes again.

'Rest now,' Jordanne told him, and kissed him once more.

They all remained a few moments more before Sister came across to do some observations. Sally indicated the door and all of them left. Returning to the tearoom, Sally crossed to the sink.

'Tea?'

'A coffee would really hit the spot,' Jordanne said with a nod.

'Nothing for me,' Jed replied.

'Alex?' Sally asked. He was standing with his back to them, looking at a picture on the wall. 'Alex?'

'Sorry,' he murmured, and turned around, a frown on his forehead.

'Would you like a drink?' She gestured to the coffee-and-tea-making facilities.

'Ah…no, thanks.'

Sally made a tea for herself and a coffee for Jordanne and

THE CONSULTANT'S CONFLICT

they all sat down at the table. Alex, though, was instantly on
his feet. 'I just remembered something I need to check on,'
he said, his words directed to Jed. 'I'll see you all later.'

'Anything I can help with?' Jed asked.

'No. No. Thanks.' With that, Alex was out of the room like
a speeding bullet.

'Is he always that…strange?' Jordanne asked with a quirky
smile.

'He's had hectic evening—retrieval team, dealing with Jed's
possessiveness over Joel, operating,' Sally listed.

'I wasn't *that* bad,' Jed protested.

'Do you want to bet on that?' Sally asked with incredulity.
'You were awful.' She laughed. Jed hung his head in mock
dejection. 'Never mind, darling,' she crooned as she placed
her arm around his shoulders and kissed his cheek. 'I still love
you.'

Jed turned his head, a smile on his lips, and kissed her.
'Good.'

'You two are so cute.' Jordanne sighed. 'When's the wedding?'

Jed held up his hand. 'We're just taking things slowly,' he
told his sister.

'Well, then, I'd better not tell you that Mum's been reading
all her cake-decorating books again.'

Jed laughed and shook his head. 'That's Mum.' He looked
at Jordanne and said, 'So where's your new apartment situ-
ated? I would have been happy to organise things for you.'

'I know, Jed, but you keep forgetting that I'm more than
capable of organising things for myself. It's actually not far
from your house. Two blocks away, in fact, and I've arranged
to pick up the keys on Monday. I have a whole week to settle
in before starting work.'

'You can still change your mind and move in with me,' Jed
offered.

'I'll accept that offer for the next two nights, but permanently?' She screwed up her nose. 'Thanks, bro, but, no,
thanks.' Jordanne smiled at him and then at Sally. 'I'm so

used to living by myself, I don't know if I could handle sharing with anyone—even my brother,' she added when Jed opened his mouth to protest.

A while later, Joel was transferred to ICU where Alex had requested he spend the night. Everyone agreed with this decision and shortly afterwards they all said goodnight to Joel. Jed and Sally checked in with the triage sister who told them that things had quietened down and to go on home. After collecting Jordanne's bags, they all bundled into Jed's car.

He drove to Sally's place and walked her inside. Jordanne stayed in the car to give them some privacy.

'This evening didn't turn out quite as planned.' Jed wrapped his arms around Sally and drew her close.

'It's only just gone one o'clock on Sunday morning. Our on-call shift isn't over yet. If another emergency comes through, we'll be seeing each other once more.'

'Let's pray there are no more emergencies,' he replied. 'For now, though, I'd better go.' He bent his head and kissed her, his lips gently nipping at her own. Neither of them deepened the kiss, they were both too exhausted. Jed raised his head and looked down into her eyes. 'Thanks for operating on Joel. It meant a lot to me, knowing that you and Alex were the ones doing the surgery.'

'Glad I was there to help,' she murmured, and rested her head against his chest.

'I'd better go,' he repeated, and drew back slightly. They walked to the door with their arms about each other, a blast of cold air hitting them after Jed had opened the door.

He kissed her once more before releasing her completely. 'Dream of me.' Jed took her hand in his and gave it a little squeeze.

'How could I not?' she replied, and their arms stretched out while Jed slowly walked backwards. Eventually the contact broke and Sally's arm dropped lifelessly back to her side. She pulled her coat around her and waved as Jed and Jordanne drove off. As she shut the door she wondered whether Jane

McElroy was *really* getting ready to make their wedding cake or whether Jordanne had just been teasing.

As Sally got ready for bed, she worried about her father. What would he say when she told him she was getting married? *And* to someone he hadn't chosen! Sally knew she was strong enough to stand up to her father—she was a qualified orthopaedic surgeon, after all—but would Jed? He still had a prejudice against wealthy people and she didn't blame him, especially since he'd told her about Anya Tolstoy. Domineering and controlling men weren't easy to handle if you didn't know how.

Pushing the thought from her mind, she switched off the bedside light and tried to concentrate on something relaxing. It was at least two a.m. before she finally fell asleep.

At the end of the following week Sally went down to the Institute, as she always did on a Friday afternoon, to do some more research for her Ph.D. The study was well under way and Sally knew that she'd definitely have it finished at the end of her year with Jed.

That was another aspect they hadn't discussed yet—what she would do when her twelve-month position ended. She hoped, with all her heart, that Jed would offer her a partnership in his practice, but nothing had been said. She guessed it was all part of his 'slow down' plan which she'd insisted upon.

She'd watched Bruce, the coach, a few times when he'd been training with various gymnasts, and she'd realised that he didn't push the other girls nearly as much as he had Alice in that one session that she'd seen. He was polite to her but that was all and she'd noticed that he tried not to be left alone with her.

This Friday, however, Bruce seemed to be more uncomfortable than usual with Sally's presence. She watched as he took young fourteen-year-old Natalie through a routine on the uneven bars. When the girl made mistakes, he just passed them off.

When Natalie's session was almost up, the side door to the room was opened and Sally looked across to see who it was.

'Alice!' Sally stood and walked towards her patient. 'What are you doing here? I haven't cleared you for training.'

'I know,' Alice said with a small smile. 'I called your consulting rooms and they said I would find you here. Which is great because I was on my way here anyway.'

'Why?'

'Come and sit down while Natalie finishes and I'll tell you all about it.'

'How's the shoulder?' Sally asked as they walked back to the seats.

'The physio is quite impressed with my rate of recovery.'

'Really?' Sally was surprised. 'Last week the physio said she thought it would take a few more months before you could come back.'

'I know, but that was before I made a deal with my father.'

'What?'

'I made a deal with my father—just like you did.'

'What's the deal?' Sally asked carefully.

'Just that he hands the responsibility for my training over to me. Bruce won't be answering to my father any more.'

'Ah.' Sally nodded. 'That explains his earlier attitude towards you. I wondered if your father was putting him under more pressure to ensure that you excelled at everything.'

'Exactly, but now things are different. I'll train again for six months and if I don't want to do it any more at the end of that time period, I don't have to.'

Sally looked at Alice's face. It was radiant with triumph. 'And...Gordon...*agreed*?'

'Eventually. I told him it was either that or I'd be leaving home immediately and giving up gymnastics all together.'

'You certainly drive a hard bargain.'

'That's what he said,' Alice said with a frown. 'Anyway, I contacted Bruce and he suggested we go over a very easy training routine—nothing to do with the arms so my shoulder can still rest but just my legs... You know, I don't want to get too stiff.'

'I don't know how that's going to go. Would it be all right if I stayed and we worked it out together—all three of us?' Sally didn't want Alice to risk any further injury.

'Actually, that's what I wanted to discuss with you.' She looked up. 'Natalie's finished. Great—let's get to it.' Alice's eyes sparkled with excitement and Sally was pleased that her patient had been able to recapture her love for the sport.

Bruce was a bit edgy to start off with but during the course of the session, he calmed down. Between the three of them, they were able to agree on a daily training regime for Alice to undertake while still protecting her shoulder from added stress.

Sally returned to her town house with a spring in her step. She was looking forward to going out tonight—with Jordanne and Kirsten. It had been ages since they'd all been together. On the other hand, she would miss spending her time with Jed. They still ate together every night but not this evening.

Her doorbell rang and she quickly crossed to open it. She gasped with surprise when she saw Jed standing there with a large bunch of bright yellow daffodils.

'Jed! They're lovely.'

'Jordanne told me they were your favourite.'

'They are.' She ushered him in and kissed him. 'Thank you.' She took them into the kitchen, and because she didn't have a vase she split the bouquet into several small ones and placed them into large glasses.

'I didn't realise you wouldn't have a vase. I would have bought one if I'd known.'

'I don't care about the vase. They're just...' Tears misted in her eyes. 'They're just lovely. So bright and cheery.'

Jed placed his arms about her. 'I can't stop for long. Alex and I decided to get together and play some cards with Joel at the hospital.'

'Good,' Sally said approvingly. She'd wondered how Jed would take her going out with the girls but he seemed perfectly all right with it. She had to keep reminding herself that he was in no way like her father. He accepted her as an individual and an equal.

'You girls have fun tonight and don't go making too much mischief.'

'*Moi?*' she questioned.

'I know how bad Jordanne can be by herself, and with two accomplices…' He left the sentence hanging.

'I haven't seen Joel since yesterday. How is he?'

'Doing well.'

'I know he felt better once he was out of ICU. And the physio?'

'All reports are excellent.'

'Terrific. Oh, by the way, I ran into Alice Partridge at the Institute.'

'Yes, Vera mentioned that she'd called the rooms, looking for you. What happened?'

Sally quickly told him what they'd achieved but didn't say anything about the niggling suspicion she had about Alice's deal with her father. Something just wasn't right there, and she was certain that Gordon wouldn't let his daughter get away with it quite so easily.

Jed stayed for a few more minutes before kissing her passionately goodnight.

'Call me when you get in,' he replied.

'Checking up on me?'

'You'd better believe it,' he said without embarrassment, and smiled at her. 'I only want to know that you're home safe because I love you.'

'I know,' she returned, and kissed him. 'Then make sure you call me if you get in first,' she added with a decisive nod.

'Will do.'

When he left, Sally had a whole ten minutes to shower and change before she was due to meet Jordanne and Kirsten at the restaurant.

They all had a wonderful evening and made a tentative date to do it again.

Sally floated through the days, knowing without a doubt that she'd never felt happier in her life. She had a great job, loyal friends and the man she loved with all her heart loved her back. What more could a woman ask for?

On Monday afternoon, Sally had just finished a very busy clinic and was looking forward to returning to Jed's place for another one of his home-cooked meals. He'd even suggested that he teach her to cook. Sally wasn't too sure how she'd go but knew under Jed's guidance it would be a whole lot of fun!

Her consulting-room door burst open, banging against the wall, and Sally looked up, startled. Her face went pale when she saw her father standing in front of her.

'Take a breath,' she whispered to herself, and tried hard to unclench her jaw. Sally lifted her chin with defiance. 'What brings you here?' She began tidying up her desk. 'Have you had some more trouble with your back again?'

'Don't be so insubordinate,' Norman Bransford growled at his daughter. 'You know damn well why I'm here. Gordon Partridge has threatened to withdraw from a joint venture unless you agree to stop pestering young Alice.'

Sally worked hard at controlling her facial expression, keeping it blank. 'I have no idea what you're talking about.'

'Stop it,' he yelled. 'You've been sticking your nose in where it doesn't belong. Gordon told me how Alice tried to make a deal with him. He knows the ridiculous way your mind works.' Norman shook his fist at her. 'If you'd done as you were told when you were a child, you wouldn't have had the opportunity to infect that poor girl's mind.'

'You mean if I'd bowed down and done your bidding? Accepted that women are the weaker sex and inferior to men?'

'Exactly.' Norman's tone and stance was a pose Sally had seen many times. He was spoiling for a good fight and she wasn't about to disappoint him.

She stood slowly and purposefully from her chair, squared her shoulders and glared back at her father. 'You have no idea, do you?'

'What are you on about? I'm stronger than you. I earn more money than you. I have more power than you.'

'And *that* makes you superior?' Sally laughed without humour. 'In the *real* world, your attitude would be called… ignorant.'

'Don't you speak to me like tha—' He yelled.

'This is *my* office,' she interrupted. 'This is *my* life. I am not a child any more. I am a grown woman—a qualified orthopaedic surgeon. I can speak to you any way I choose.'

'I'll cut you off without a cent,' Norman threatened.

'I thought you'd already done that. Don't you see? I'm not *interested* in your money. I don't *want* your money.'

'You're delusional,' he blustered. 'Typical female. You have no idea what you're on about.'

'I know exactly what I'm on about,' she stated calmly, which angered her father all the more. As a doctor, Sally had worked hard to control the temper she knew she'd inherited from her father. 'I've successfully managed to divert you from the topic you came here to discuss.'

'Nonsense,' he growled, and shoved his hands into his pockets.

'Excuse me,' a deep voice said from the doorway, and both Sally and Norman turned to see Jed standing there. 'Would you mind lowering your voice? This is a medical practice.' He directed his words at Norman who gave Jed a cursory glance before dismissing him.

'You keep away from Alice Partridge,' Norman threatened Sally again.

'And if I don't?' Sally enquired, interested to see what he'd say.

Jed took a few steps into the room, positioning himself between Norman and Sally. He glared down at Sally's father, his gaze filled with contempt. Indicating the door, he said in a menacing tone that brooked no argument, 'Leave. *Now.*'

Norman Bransford looked him over with a sneer on his face. 'What right—' Norman spat the word '—do *you* have to speak to *me* like that?'

'The right that states, if you don't leave, I'll have you charged with trespassing,' Jed replied coolly.

'Ugh,' he heard Sally groan from behind him. Jed didn't move. He kept his gaze glued on Norman Bransford—a man he despised on sight. Moments later Sally walked from the room, grabbing her coat from the hook by the door. She didn't stop to look at them and Jed had a gut feeling that he'd just annoyed the woman of his dreams. He'd call her later—right now, though, he had Norman Bransford to deal with.

Once Sally had left the room Norman's stance changed. He relaxed a little—a ploy to get Jed to do the same. He looked slowly around the room before saying, 'Nice set-up you have. Looks as though things could do with a bit of a touch-up here and there—new carpets, paint,' he suggested.

Jed simply stood staring at Norman.

'I need a bit of help in getting Sally to back down from pestering young Alice Partridge. So how would one hundred thousand go towards modernising this place? Two hundred thousand?' he offered when Jed didn't reply.

'Three hundred thousand.' Norman pulled a chequebook and pen from his inside coat pocket and opened it.

Jed's fingers automatically curled themselves into a fist and he had to work hard at controlling his temper. How dare Norman Bransford think he could waltz in here, upset Sally and start bribing people?

'Five hundred thousand?' Norman queried at Jed's silence. 'You drive a hard bargain.' He laughed casually as he began writing out the cheque.

'You're wasting your ink because there's no way I'll ever accept any money from you,' Jed fumed. 'There's no way *any* member of my family will *ever* accept a bribe from you. You should have known that when my sister Jordanne turned you down all those years ago.'

'Who?' Norman asked, his brow furrowing into a frown.

'Typical. You've probably bought so many people off you can't distinguish one from the other,' Jed finished with disgust.

'So you're refusing to help me,' Norman stated matter-of-factly. He exhaled slowly and peered more closely at Jed. 'What are your intentions towards my daughter?' he drawled.

'Absolutely none of your business,' Jed ground out.

'You can't only be interested in her as a colleague. She's an attractive woman.'

Norman's words made Jed sick to the stomach. Was that all he thought of his own daughter? Was she only someone beautiful to look at? A decoration? Why wouldn't a man be interested in Sally for her brains? Jed knew *he* certainly was. Until Sally, he'd *never* found a woman who was his equal in every way—physically, spiritually and intellectually.

'So that's why you were holding out for more money,' Norman continued when Jed didn't respond. 'You like the way she looks so you need more of an incentive to do what I'm asking. How much do you want? Name your price.'

'My price is way too high, even for you.'

'I doubt that.' Norman preened. 'I'm *extremely* rich.'

'You…can't…buy…me.' Jed said each word slowly and clearly as though he were talking to an imbecile.

'Everyone has their price,' Norman persisted. 'One million dollars.'

'Is that all your daughter's worth?'

'One and a half million.' Norman shrugged nonchalantly. 'I can afford it.'

Jed shook his head in contempt. 'My price—'

'Now we're getting somewhere,' Norman said with enthusiasm.

'Is that you leave Sally alone for the rest of her life,' Jed continued.

Norman looked at Jed before laughing without humour. 'You've fallen in love with her. You—' he sneered at Jed '—weak-minded wimp.'

Jed bristled and had to hold himself back from reaching over and slugging Norman Bransford right in the face. 'Get out.' Jed's low growl was filled with contempt and disgust at the man before him.

Their gazes clashed before Norman slowly put his chequebook away. He didn't say a word as he turned and walked through the open door of Sally's consulting room. Jed stood where he was, listening for the outer door of the clinic to close.

'Lock the door,' he called to Vera. When heard the click he closed his eyes and breathed in a deep and fulfilling breath. He'd rejected Anya Tolstoy's father's attempts to buy him and he'd just repeated the scenario with Norman Bransford. When would these people learn that some human beings had integrity?

Sally didn't answer her phone that night and when Jed came around, knocking on her door, she told him to go away.

'You're obviously still mad at me,' he called from the other side of the door.

'Mad? No. I'm furious,' she returned.

'Then let me in and let's discuss things.'

When she didn't reply he continued, 'Come on, Sally. It's freezing out here.'

He had a point, she rationalised. Even though she hadn't asked him to come, she couldn't let him freeze. She unlocked the door and stepped away, standing in the middle of the room, her eyes blazing with burning anger, her hands planted firmly on her hips.

Jed shut the door behind him and looked at her. 'Can I take my coat off before round one begins?'

'Don't try to be cute or funny, Jed McElroy. What you did today was inexcusable.'

Jed shrugged out of his coat and hung it up. He took a step towards her but Sally held up her hand.

'I'd keep your distance if I were you. With the way I'm feeling, you're likely to get a fist in your stomach. How could you interfere like that?'

'Like what?' Jed spread his arms wide, indicating he wasn't sure what she was talking about.

'I've told you before, Jed. I can handle my father. I've dealt with him for years and I was doing just fine before you barged into my room to protect the ''poor little woman''.'

'First of all, I didn't *barge* in—the door was wide open.

Secondly, he was creating a disturbance in the building I own. Regardless of how you feel, I had every right to intervene.'

'Regardless of how I feel? That's *exactly* what I'm talking about. I've been dominated by him my entire life, *my* feelings were of no consequence. This is the *last* thing I need now.' She took a breath and looked at him, lowering her voice. 'You have to realise that I can look after myself—fight my own battles. I've done pretty well with my father so far and I can handle anything he throws at me. I'm a tough cookie. I don't need your protection, Jed, especially from my father. I completely resent what you did today. Positioning yourself between the two of us, looking down at him. You've only made matters worse.'

'I rejected his offers,' Jed informed her.

Sally looked at him and shook her head in amazement. 'Do you honestly believe it's over? My father stands to lose a couple of billion dollars unless he can assure Gordon Partridge that Alice will always do as she's told. Men like my father and Gordon *need* to have complete control of every situation and person around them. By bringing yourself into the firing line today, my father will now want control over you as well.'

'But I rejected his offer,' Jed stated again.

Sally sighed and raked a hand through her hair, her anger almost dissipated. 'You probably should have accepted it.'

'*What?*' Jed looked at her with incredulity. 'Are you out of your mind?' He took a step forward and Sally didn't object. 'I could *never* accept…pay-off money…from anyone, and especially *not* a man like your father.'

'You don't get it, Jed. He works on tactics. Everything is a tactic. Everything he says, does—every minute action—is a tactic.' Sally turned and walked to the lounge where she sank down into the comfortable cushions, her fingers rubbing her forehead as she began to think things through. 'He'll make you another offer. When he does, see how high you can get him to go and then accept it.'

'No. I could *never* do that.'

'*Think* about it, Jed. You don't have to really take the money—just let him write a cheque so he thinks he's won.'

'That won't solve anything,' Jed countered. 'Besides, it would be going against all my principles. You can't ask me to do that.'

'You're right,' she agreed after a moment's silence. 'Sorry. Sometimes he drives me…just so insane. I'm always trying to second-guess what he's going to do next so I can be prepared for anything.' Sally sighed in frustration.

Jed took Sally's hand in his. 'Are we OK now?'

Sally looked at him but didn't withdraw her hand. 'I'm still mad at you. You've played the protective big brother all your life and naturally, given your feelings for me, those instincts envelop me as well. But I'm different from your siblings, Jed. I've been brought up in a society and manner that you can't even begin to truly understand. Please, just accept the fact that I can handle my father and next time let me deal with him.'

Jed was silent and Sally saw his jaw clenching.

'Promise me, Jed,' she pressed.

He was silent again before finally saying, 'I can't.'

Sally dropped her hand and frowned. 'Why not?'

'Sally.' He sat down next to her. 'I love you and my first instinct is not to allow anyone to upset or harm you. I can't change who I am just because I don't understand your up-bringing. I don't want *anyone*, not even your father, not the Gordon Partridges of this world—*anyone*—to treat you the way you've been treated. It's not right.'

'You can't just waltz into my life and start changing things around to suit yourself.'

'That's not what I meant.'

'That's how it came across.'

'Sally, we've come from different backgrounds and because of that there's a lot of…adjustment that has to take place when two people like us start seriously dating. I admire the fact that you've stood up to your father and succeeded in your chosen career path, but what I'm saying *now* is that you're no longer alone. I *support* you and, in doing so, I don't want anyone to hurt you.'

'If you support me, Jed, then let me deal with him.'

Jed thought about this for a moment. 'I'll never accept pay-offs from him,' he said with a stony expression.

'I understand,' Sally said with a nod. 'So you'll let me handle him?'

Jed wrapped his arms about her. 'I'll try and follow your lead. That's all I can promise for now.'

Jed stayed and cooked them both dinner, urging Sally to join him for her first lesson. Sally knew both of them were putting on a happy front and that things weren't really completely settled. The matter couldn't be, until her father left them alone.

On Friday Jed was late in for the morning clinic, and when she left to go to the Institute he was consulting with a patient. Sally watched Alice and a few other gymnasts train before heading to the library.

She'd decided against telling Alice all that had transpired on Norman's visit. The young athlete had a smile on her face and a spring in her step. The weight of a domineering father had been lifted from her shoulders and Sally noticed great improvement in the simple routines they'd arranged for her to do while her shoulder was still healing.

Sally pushed open the library door and was greeted warmly by Sky, the librarian.

'Hi. I've managed to get those journals in you were after.'

'Fantastic.' Sally smiled at her. 'Thank you.'

'Hey, it's all part of my job. They're here somewhere…' The librarian bent behind the counter and Sally could hear her shuffling things around.

Sally waited.

'Oh, and, of course, you've heard the latest news…' Sky mumbled.

'What news is that?' Sally asked.

'About the new equipment for the biodome.'

'Do you mean Jed actually found someone to pay for it all? He's been trying to raise the funds for quite some time.'

'Well, apparently, some big business hotshot has donated everything required to the biodome *because* of Jed.'

Sally felt prickles of wariness spread throughout her body and the smile disappeared from her face. She shook her head, trying desperately to clear away the dawning realisation that was encompassing her.

'Do…do…um…?' Sally cleared her suddenly dry throat. 'Do we know who the donor was?'

'Found them,' Sky called triumphantly, and brought the journals up to the counter. 'Sorry?'

'The hotshot who donated it. Do we know who he is?' Sally tried to keep her tone from bordering on impatient.

Sky frowned. 'Barnsfield? Brandon? Something like that. I can't remember. What I *do* know is that he was impressed with Jed's research and dedication to the project, which is why he decided to hand over the money.'

'Who told you this?'

'Bill did. You've met him, haven't you? He's one of the biomedical engineers who works in the biodome.'

'When does the equipment arrive?'

'On Monday! Can you believe it? Bill thought it would have taken at least a fortnight, if not a month, to get it here but, nope, it arrives on Monday.'

'When was this announced?' Sally knew she was asking a lot of questions but she couldn't help it. Her intuition was working in overdrive and she desperately needed confirmation.

'There was a press conference this morning. Apparently Jed was there and the media and everything. It should be in to-morrow's paper. Exciting, isn't it?' Sky bubbled over with happiness.

'Jed *knows* about this?'

'Of course he does.' Sky looked at Sally and frowned in concentration before snapping her fingers in remembrance. 'Bransford.'

'Yes?' Sally answered cautiously.

'That was his name—the man who donated the equipment. Any relation?'

Sally closed her eyes in anguish, desperately trying to control her breathing. 'My father,' she whispered between clenched teeth.

'*Really?* Wow! You *are* full of surprises. Gold medallist, wealthy parents.' Sky faltered for a moment as Sally opened her eyes. 'Are you all right?'

Sally tried to unclench her jaw before forcing a smile. 'Fine. Everything's just fine. Uh…thanks again for the journals.'

'OK. See you next week.'

Sally stormed out of the library and headed towards her car. The rain had started to fall once more but she strode purposefully forward, not caring whether she got wet. How could Jed *do* this to her? How could he accept the equipment when it was obviously pay-off money?

Sally forced herself to drive the short distance back to the clinic carefully.

'Is someone with him?' Sally asked Vera on her way down the corridor.

'No, he's just finished,' Vera replied.

Sally didn't even bother to knock on his door but pushed it open and walked right up to his desk, her eyes blazing with fury.

'I see you've heard,' he said when he looked up from what he was typing.

'How could you?'

'Sally—'

'I thought I explained things quite clearly to you the other day. Now my father has you right where he wants you and there's absolutely nothing you can do about it. So what are you going to do? Take me off Alice's case now and let Gordon control her again?'

'Just wait a minute,' Jed returned, and stood, his desk still between them. 'Your father does not have me anywhere.'

'Oh, no? The papers tomorrow will confirm it. You have no idea how manipulative he can be.'

'What was I supposed to do—turn around and walk out?'

'That might have helped.'

'Norman had the entire press throughout the ACT and NSW there. I didn't know a thing about it.'

'It doesn't matter what your honourable intentions were—the fact remains that he has you in his pocket. If you don't do exactly what he wants now, Jed, he will ruin your career. Believe me, he can. He's done it to people before and he'll do it again.'

'You're overreacting.'

'Oh, no, I'm not. Don't you see? Men like my father have all sorts of people owing them favours. People very high up on medical boards and now, in this instance, I'm almost positive he has the powers that be on the governing board at the Institute willing to do whatever he wants. It's the same situation as your friend Anya Tolstoy.'

'What?' Jed looked at her with disbelief. 'This is nothing like that situation.'

'Oh, come off it, Jed. Anya's father realised he couldn't get to you but he certainly managed to get to Anya—the proof of that is in her marrying that other man.'

'What are you talking about?'

'Anya's father would have blackmailed her with *your* career, your status as a professional. He would have ruined you if she hadn't done things his way, which is exactly what she did. If you'd simply walked back out of that press conference, you would have at least had your integrity, regardless of whatever else my father would have done to you. It's the same ploy, except my father isn't going behind your back as Tolstoy did. My father is blackmailing you in public—for all the world to see. You know how incredible our biodome is. We have specialists and professionals coming from all over the world to see it. We have the best international athletes coming to try it out. This piece of news won't be just local or even national, it will be international.'

When she'd finished, she looked at him fairly and squarely. Jed's gaze, however, was stony. 'How dare you imply that I have no integrity?' His voice held a strong thread of disgust. 'All you're concerned with is the fact that he's supposedly won. You think he has me in his pocket and now I'll roll over and do whatever it is that he wants. Well, *you're* wrong, Sally. *Very* wrong.

'I'll tell you what I really think. I think you're more annoyed with *yourself* because you didn't see this coming. I think you enjoy these little games with your father. You both play to win. You both manipulate and coerce the people around you so that things always turn out your way.'

Sally's jaw dropped open at his words.

'You've said that you know how to handle him, but he certainly knows how to handle you.' Jed's voice held a hint of contempt. 'You said I'd never understand your upbringing and you're right, but what I *do* understand is that you're much more like your father than you'd ever admit to. You're stubborn, pig-headed and manipulative, as well as wanting to be in control—all the time and of every situation. The other day, when he confronted you in your office, you didn't like my intervention because *you* weren't in control.'

Sally shook her head, her eyes misting with tears. Her breathing increased and the fury that buzzed through her veins at his words was mixed with disbelief that he could actually say such horrible things to her.

Clenching her teeth, Sally managed to suppress her feelings for a moment. 'If you honestly believe everything you've said, then I guess…I guess you don't…love me after all.' With that she turned and ran out of the room, through the building and down to her car. Wiping the tears from her eyes, she started the engine and drove. She didn't want to go home, she didn't want to see or speak to anyone. How could Jed say such awful things to her? He didn't know how terrible her father could be. He didn't understand the situation at all and it was obviously pointless explaining it to him. She'd thought Jed loved her. *Really* loved her. Who was she trying to kid? He didn't even *trust* her, let alone love her. It had all been an enormous mistake.

Sally vowed right then and there *never* to allow herself to become vulnerable to anyone *ever* again.

She continued to drive, unsure of where she'd end up.

CHAPTER TEN

'WOULD you like something more to eat, dear?' Jane McElroy asked Sally.

'No, thank you.'

'Drink? Another cup of tea perhaps? Slice of toast? Orange juice?'

'No, thank you.' Sally smiled up at Jed's mother. Her car had almost driven itself to his parents' place yesterday evening and she'd been welcomed with open arms. Neither Jane nor John had pressed her to talk about why she was there, they'd simply accepted her.

'Why don't you go and have a nice relaxing bath? Jordanne leaves clothes here when she stays, so feel free to wear them.'

Sally nodded. 'Thank you.' Tears welled in her eyes at Jane's kindness.

'Oh, you're very welcome, dear.' Jane placed her arm around Sally shoulders and gave them a little squeeze. 'I'm so glad you've come to visit. Let me go and get that bath organised for you while you take a look through Jordanne's clothes. You'll find them in the room you slept in last night.'

Sally rose from the small kitchen table, where Jane and her husband ate when on their own, and returned to the lovely pink room. It had ballerinas and flowers on the walls. The single bed was covered with frills and lace—in every essence, a little girl's room. One that had been decorated with love. Sally's room had been filled to the brim with soft cuddly animals, the latest toys and anything else her parents had thought she should have. No one had ever *asked* her what she'd wanted yet Sally could quite easily see Jordanne standing in the room, helping her father paste the wallpaper into place. Or picking out the material for her bedspread and helping her mother sew it.

Sally sat down on the bed and cried the tears that had been unable to fall last night. Her entire life had been devoid of love and just when she'd thought she'd found it with Jed, that, too, had turned out to be just another mirage. She snuggled down in the bed, just as Jordanne would have done every night, being kissed lovingly by her parents and told to have sweet dreams. While Sally had been sent to bed by one of the many strict nannies who had all been controlled by her father. No kisses, not even a cuddle. They weren't permitted in her family because her father thought emotion, and particularly open displays of it, made a person weak.

Hugging the bedcovers closely around her, Sally sobbed into the material. She cried for her past, her present and her future without Jed. Never before, in her entire life, had she felt so desolate—so alone—as she did right now. The poor little rich girl.

She cried until her eyes were puffy, her face red and blotchy and her body aching from the pressure of the racking sobs that convulsed her. Her head pounded and the ringing in her ears wouldn't stop.

Eventually, her breathing slowed and became deeper with only the occasional hiccup. She drifted off into a deep sleep where her dreams of Jed were so confused they blurred into one big mass of images.

'Sally?'

She heard her name being called and she turned in the direction it had come from. It was a sweet voice, calming, and she saw an angel in white floating above her.

'Sally, dear,' the voice called softly again. The angel blurred and then disappeared when Sally roused from her sleep and opened her eyes.

'I'm sorry to wake you,' Jane crooned, as though Sally were one of her own precious children. Oh, how she wished it were true.

Sally was focusing more clearly, but when she tried to sit

up the pounding in her head returned. 'Ooh.' Sally screwed her eyes shut and rested her head back on the pillow.

'I thought you might have a headache. Would you like some paracetamol?'

'Yes, please,' Sally whispered, her eyes still closed. When Jane returned with a glass of water and the paracetamol, Sally gratefully swallowed the tablets.

'What time is it?' Sally asked as she glanced at the closed curtains.

'It's almost seven-thirty on Saturday night.'

'I've slept all day?' Sally was alarmed at the prospect. 'I'm so sorry.'

'Don't you dare apologise. You obviously needed the rest. I only woke you because I thought you should eat something. Dinner's almost ready and afterwards I'd like you to get into the bath and relax. Then you can read a book, watch television or just go back to sleep. Your poor body appears to be crying out for a bit of pampering.'

Sally didn't know what to say but surmised that Jane was probably right.

'Get changed into something a bit more comfortable,' Jane suggested as she stood up and walked to the door. 'We'll see you downstairs soon.'

When Jane had left, Sally stayed where she was for a few moments. Sally could feel the tears once more threaten to fill her eyes at the other woman's kindness. How she desperately wished that the McElroys were her *real* family. That she and Jed were married, making her one of the close-knit clan.

Summoning up a breath of courage, Sally pushed the covers back and slowly sat up on the side of the bed. She looked down at the crumpled clothes she'd been wearing since yesterday morning. Her tailored black trousers and soft royal blue silk shirt were crushed and creased to oblivion. She felt gritty and stale in them. Following Jane's advice, she crossed to the wardrobe and opened the doors. There wasn't much to choose from but there was enough.

As Sally changed, she was thankful that she and Jordanne

were a similar size, even though Sally was a tiny bit taller than her friend. Last night, when she'd arrived, she'd been too exhausted to do anything except lie down on the bed and fall asleep.

Choosing one of Jordanne's fleecy tracksuits and a pair of warm, comfortable socks, Sally brushed her hair and looked at her reflection in the mirror. Her face was withdrawn and tired, her eyes had bags beneath them and her lips were pressed together in an effort to control her emotions.

'You don't look crash hot,' she told herself, then shrugged. She'd been brought up with the tradition that appearance—image—was everything. She'd soon learned at med school that it wasn't the be-all and end-all of living. Still, it had taken quite a long time for Sally not to care if a hair was out of place.

'Good to see you,' John McElroy welcomed her as she walked into the kitchen. 'May I get you a drink?' he asked.

He sounded so much like his son that Sally stared at him for a moment before answering. 'Mineral or soda water would be great, thank you.' She forced a smile.

'Here you go, dear,' Jane said as she placed a plate in front of Sally. 'I haven't given you too much, but if you want some more there's plenty.'

'One thing Jane has found difficult to do,' John told her after pouring her drink, 'is to stop cooking for everyone.'

'I've been so used to cooking for a large family that as the number of children decreased I had trouble halving my recipes.'

There was general chit-chat over dinner. No one mentioned Jed's name at all and Sally was thankful. After dinner Jane sent her off for a bath and Sally didn't argue. This time, though, she didn't fall asleep as she'd done that morning when Jane had suggested she relax in a bath, and instead lay in the warm, bubbly water trying to figure out when she'd allowed herself the luxury of a soak in the tub. The answer was—never! Not like this.

Sally slept soundly that night, her dreams of Jed containing more of the happier times they'd shared, and in the morning woke feeling like a new person. She was up, showered and dressed before seven a.m., as was her custom when working. She made herself tea and toast, not feeling self-conscious of doing it in someone else's kitchen, before heading out onto the back verandah.

She sat down at the outdoor table which had been brought beneath the shelter for the winter weather. The rain teemed down and the wind was cool, but it wasn't icy. Sally returned inside, found a blanket by the door and took it out with her. Wrapping herself up, she ate her breakfast with a renewed outlook on her life. Now that she'd had a good night's sleep, Sally felt as though she could cope once more.

She was determined to put things right with Jed. It didn't matter what it would take, there was no way she was going to lose him. He meant far too much to her. He was her one true love—her soul mate.

She'd finished her toast and was on her second cup of tea when Jane came out to find her.

'There you are, dear. I was a little worried when I checked your room to find you gone. You're looking so much better today.'

'I'm feeling it. Thank you.'

'We've done nothing, dear,' Jane replied as she sat next to Sally.

'Here.' Sally unfolded the blanket. 'Stay warm with me.'

They both sat there beneath the blanket and looked out at the rain.

'The garden's looking so beautiful and green,' Jane remarked. 'Although I confess that spring is my favourite season, when all the flowers are in bloom.'

'Mine, too.' Sally smiled. She waited a while before saying, 'You and John have been so wonderful. Thank you for not pressuring me.'

'It does no good,' Jane replied. 'We've had six children to raise and you learn soon enough just to be there. Support and love can help carry people through a crisis, making them stronger once they've been through it.'

'I'm ready to talk,' Sally said softly.

'And I'm ready to listen,' Jane said, and smiled at her.

'I'm not sure where to begin.' Sally's voice wobbled a bit and Jane found her hand and squeezed it.

'Start at the beginning. Tell me about your parents. How did they meet?'

'My maternal grandfather and my father were in business together. I guess it was a merger of sorts but my mother has always doted on my father. She told me once that she knows he has his faults but she loves him nevertheless.'

'You sound as though you don't approve?'

'Ugh, you don't know him.'

'So tell me.'

Sally hesitated for a brief moment before telling Jane about her childhood and how her father had manipulated and controlled her. She explained that she understood how her father had turned out that way, due to his own upbringing by a man who had been dictatorial and manipulative.

'Yet you've broken the cycle.'

'Hmm. Jed wouldn't seem to think so. He told me I'm just like my father, that I like to be in control of every situation—and I guess he had a point.' Sally looked down at the pattern on the blanket, not really seeing it at all.

'You and Jed are a perfect match, in my opinion, and I have no doubt that you'll work things out. I love my son but I can also see things from your point of view. Remember I told you that I was an only child? When you don't have parents or siblings to rely on, you tend to get used to doing things your way. It's not that you're not good at sharing, it's just that you've never really had to put it into practice. Living with siblings is different from sharing your pencils with your friends at school or swapping clothes every now and then with a friend.

'It's been a constant source of enlightenment for me to watch the way my children love, honour and protect each other. Of course, there were small spats here and there but nothing major. They continued to offer support and encouragement through every aspect of each other's lives.'

'It sounds wonderful,' Sally breathed.

'It was very hard for me in the beginning, though. John had two brothers and a sister. His oldest brother has died but he still keeps in close contact with the rest of his family. John wanted to get involved with my life, to help me through things. I finally realised that if we were to become *one* in a marriage, I had to let him into my life. Equally. You've probably been taught that leaning on someone is a sign of weakness, yet look at the time you've spent here. You've leaned on John and me, rested and relaxed your body, soul and mind, and now aren't you feeling better?'

'Yes.'

'You won't lose your independence and neither will Jed lose his. Not if you're *equally* dependent upon each other.'

'I understand what you're saying, Jane, but there's more to it than that,' Sally said, before explaining the whole story about how her father was trying to blackmail the two of them.

Jane listened in silence and when Sally was finished she asked, 'How did you feel about your paternal grandfather?'

The question caught Sally a little off guard. 'Well, I…um…didn't really have much to do with him until he became sick with emphysema.'

'Did he contact you?'

'No. When I learned through my father's secretary that he was ill both Mum and I went to see him. I was shell-shocked. I'd never seen him like that—all happy and smiles. I was wary at first but after a while I realised he was genuine. It was in my last year of med school, and not long after I graduated he died.'

'You reconciled your differences with him and that made you feel…how?'

'Um…well, happy.'

'So think of how things will be if you can reconcile with your father.'

'That's different, Jane. My grandfather was *willing* to change, to admit to his mistakes, to take responsibility for his actions. Do you know he gave away his entire fortune in those last six months of his life and that the estate he lived in is now used as a nursing home for other patients with emphysema?'

'Yes. I remember reading about it in the paper at the time.'

'My father isn't willing to do anything like that. He's still focused on power and control.'

'Yet you told me he's threatened to cut you out of his will several times but hasn't. What do you think *that* means?'

'I'm not sure,' Sally replied softly. 'I've lived without any support, financial or otherwise, from him for years now.'

'And still he finds little ways to contact you, burst into your life.'

'He's just trying to control me again.'

'Is he?'

Sally thought about all those times when he'd tried to buy her placements at hospitals and how she'd ruthlessly turned them down, refusing to accept any help from him. Maybe it had been his way of getting her attention. She'd told Jed countless times that she knew how best to handle her father, but perhaps she'd been wrong. Could this situation with Alice be another ploy for her father to work his way back into her life? Sally desperately wanted to believe it, but years of experience had taught her to harden her heart.

'He was *never* there when I was growing up,' she protested.

'You said he'd wanted a son. Perhaps he didn't know *how* to relate to a daughter. I'm not trying to justify what he's done, Sally, I'm only trying to help you see things from a different perspective. Please, I urge you not to have any regrets in your life. Don't wait until things go wrong before trying to fix them. Take the step, the initiative, and stretch out your hands to both your parents. I think you might be surprised.'

'What about Jed?'

'Believe me, dear, you and Jed are fine.'

'How can you say that? We're not even talking.'

'There are many different ways to communicate and, let me tell you, kissing and making up is the best part of any argument.'

Sally looked puzzled for a moment before asking, 'He knows I'm here, doesn't he?'

'Yes. He called on Friday night, frantic with worry. You pulled up in the driveway while John was still on the phone to him. He called twice that evening to check on you and several times yesterday. He understands you needed time to think everything through and is glad you felt you could turn to us—as are we. Jed loves you so much, Sally, and I know this because he's *never* been so out of control in his life.' Jane lifted her hands above the blanket and brought them slowly together, spreading her fingers wide. Only the fingertips were touching—the left thumb to the right thumb, the left index finger to the right index finger and so on right down to the little finger on each hand. 'This, to me, is marriage. Two people, both separate identities, coming together to lean upon each other equally, completely interdependent yet still individuals. You and Jed need to loosen your control on your individual lives and lean on each other. When Joel had his accident Jed leaned on you and you let him. Didn't it feel wonderful?'

'Yes.' Sally nodded for emphasis and smiled at the memory.

'Let Jed in, Sally, so he, too, can have that feeling of giving to you. Equal taking, equal receiving. If one is out of balance, then you need to readjust your alignment to centre it again.'

'It's hard,' Sally said after a while. 'I've never relied on anyone but myself.'

'I know, dear, but take the step. Communication, remember.'

John came out onto the verandah with the portable phone in his hand. 'Sorry to intrude.' His face was grim. 'Jed's on the phone. He needs to speak to you urgently.'

John held the phone out to Sally who took it with trembling hands.

She cleared her throat and took a deep breath. 'Hello.'

'Sally.' The way he said her name was a caress and one

she desperately needed. She closed her eyes momentarily, savouring the sensation.

'I wish I could call you under better circumstances.'

Her eyes snapped open and she stared straight ahead, concentrating hard. 'Jed? What's happened?' Every nerve ending in her body was on alert.

'It's your father. He's been involved in a bad car accident. They've just taken him to Canberra General in an ambulance.'

CHAPTER ELEVEN

FROM then on, everything seemed to pass in a blur for Sally. Jed had told her that he'd had another meeting with her father that Sunday morning and a few minutes after Norman had left there'd been the sound of twisted metal.

'A semi-trailer had lost its brakes, went through a red light and smashed directly into your father's car.'

When Jed had given her a possible list of fractures, Sally was shocked. Almost every major bone in her father's body had been broken. She contacted her mother and told her what had happened. For some reason, Sally had expected her mother to fall apart at the seams, yet Beatrice Bransford had surprised her daughter by taking clear and decisive action.

Beatrice arranged to collect Sally on her way to the airport where one of the Bransford Corporation planes would fly them to Canberra. Sally checked with John and Jane that it was all right to leave her car with them.

'You go, dear,' Jane said, enveloping her in a warm hug. John reached down and kissed her cheek. 'Don't fret about the car.'

A large black limousine pulled up outside the front of the house. 'That'll be Mum.' She picked up her coat and work bag before turning to smile warmly at Jed's parents. 'Thank you—both—so much. The past couple of days have been wonderful.'

'You're more than welcome,' John said with a nod. 'Let us know what happens with your dad.'

'Of course,' she replied.

John quickly opened the door and Sally gave Jane another hug. 'Thanks,' she whispered in Jane's ear, before hurrying to the waiting car.

'They look like nice people,' Beatrice remarked as Sally climbed in and sat down opposite her mother.

'They are.' She wound down the window and waved as the car pulled away.

'You're not looking too good at the moment,' Beatrice commented after a few minutes of silence.

Sally looked down at her clothes, about to explain her lack of perfect attire to her mother. Jordanne's old denim jeans and baggy home-knitted jumper might not have been the latest designer fashions but Sally felt more comfortable in them than anything she had in her own wardrobe.

'Really, Mother?' she asked with a large smile. 'That's funny because I *feel* quite good.'

'Because your father has had an accident?' Beatrice asked rather drolly.

'No!' Sally was horrified that her mother could even think such a thing. 'No. All I meant was that for the first time in my life I'm beginning to find out who I really am.'

The look in Beatrice's eyes softened a little. 'I'm…happy for you, Sally.'

'Thanks.'

'So tell me more about your father's accident.'

'I've already told you what I know.' Sally pulled her mobile phone from her bag and dialled Jed's number. She only received his answering service. Leaving a message to let him know her plans, she ended the call saying, 'I love you. See you soon.'

'Who's that?' Beatrice asked.

'Jed McElroy.'

'Jordanne's brother?' Beatrice was surprised.

'Yes.'

'But he's your boss, isn't he?'

'Yes.' Sally was quite surprised at herself. She didn't feel at all apologetic or self-conscious about admitting to loving Jed.

'You really *are* getting to know yourself.' Beatrice reached across and squeezed her daughter's hand. It was the first sign

of affection Sally had received from her mother in years.
'Come and sit by me.'

Sally did as she was asked.

'Now, explain what you know of your father's injuries to
me.'

'Well, Jed could only give me a rough guide of his injuries
as everything was still to be confirmed with the X-rays. His
pelvis is probably fractured in a few places, he's broken both
of his legs and arms, cracked quite a few ribs, broken a few
fingers and was unconscious at the accident site, which may
indicate a head injury.'

Beatrice bit her lower lip but took a calming breath. 'This
means he'll be out of action for quite a while, doesn't it?'

'Yes. I guess he'll be able to do some work from his bedside, but that wouldn't be for at least four weeks. It all depends
on the X-rays. Jed said he couldn't tell if his spinal column
was damaged. If it is...' Sally let her sentence trail off.

Beatrice picked up the phone in the car and dialled a number. 'Rupert?' she asked, and waited for an answer. 'It's
Beatrice. Cancel all of Norman's meetings for the next six
weeks.' There was a pause. 'Stop blustering and listen,'
Beatrice said firmly but calmly. 'You're Norman's personal
secretary and right-hand man. He's been involved in a serious
car accident. I'm currently on my way to Canberra. There's
no need to cause alarm within the company at this stage so
make whatever excuse you need to cancel his meetings. I'll
keep you informed.'

When Beatrice had disconnected the call, Sally smiled and
nodded. 'Good for you, Mum.'

'Norman needs me,' she whispered, her eyes filling with
tears. 'Now more than ever.'

During the rest of their trip Sally and Beatrice spoke more
than they'd ever done, and when they arrived at Canberra
General they both marched into A and E with confident steps.

'Sally?' The receptionist greeted her with surprise. 'They're
all still in Theatre. Go through to the tearoom.'

'Which theatre?'

'Emergency one.'

'Thanks. This way, Mum.'

The instant they rounded the corner into the tearoom, Sally picked up the phone and dialled the theatre extension. When the scout nurse answered she said, 'I'd like to speak to Jed, please. It's Sally.'

'Right away, Dr Bransford,' the nurse replied.

A few moments later Jed's voice came down the line. 'I received your message. I presume you're in the hospital?'

'That's right.'

'I'll come out.'

Sally disconnected the call and prowled around the room.

'Tea would be nice,' Beatrice remarked.

'Sorry, Mum.' Sally crossed to the sink. 'How do you take it?'

'I wasn't asking you to wait on me,' Beatrice said as she came to stand by her daughter. 'Believe it or not, I'm more than capable of making my own tea. Let me get you a cup, Sally.'

'No. I'm not thirsty. I just need to see...' She turned expectantly as the tearoom door opened. Ian Parks, one of Alex's registrars, came into the room. Sally closed her eyes and sighed in exasperation.

'Hi, Sally,' he greeted her. 'Sorry to hear about your dad. What's the news?'

'I don't know. I'm waiting for Jed to come out of Theatre.'

'Ah. That explains your look when I came in just now.' Ian crossed to the sink and helped himself to a cup of coffee. He introduced himself to Beatrice and once again offered his support for her husband. 'I've just finished operating on the other MVA patient, the one who crashed into your father.'

'What? What happened?' Sally asked.

'He died,' Ian said solemnly.

'*What?*' both Sally and Beatrice said in unison.

'On impact, he was thrown from the cabin of his truck and run over by a passing car. He suffered extensive internal bleeding as well as multiple fractures. I fixed his fractured femur and the general surgeons tried to patch him up, but to no avail.' Ian shook his head and sighed. 'The damage was too great.'

'And the car that ran over him? Where is that person?' Beatrice asked with concern.

'The last I heard they'd been treated for shock and discharged.'

'If it's possible…' Beatrice turned to face her daughter '…I'd like the personal details of that person as well as the truck driver's family. Any legal costs, medical bills, counselling sessions—they'll all be covered by the Bransford Corporation.'

Sally had never seen her mother like this before—a woman in charge. 'Certainly. We can't give out personal details but I can have the hospital arrange for all payments to be covered.'

'I want those people to have the best care they can receive,' Beatrice stressed.

'I'll get onto that right away,' Ian said as he drained his coffee-cup and took it to the sink.

'I'll wash that,' Beatrice told him. 'It will give me something to do.'

'Thanks,' Ian said, and left them alone.

Sally put her hand on her mother's shoulder. 'You seem to be holding up well.'

'Norman needs me,' she stated. 'I'm determined to be strong for him. If he sees me weeping and worrying then it will impede his recovery.'

'Just don't bottle up everything inside,' Sally suggested. 'We have some great social workers who are more than willing to have you bend their ear.'

'I'll keep it in mind,' Beatrice said with a nod.

'Sally!'

She turned at the sound of her name and rushed across the room, flinging herself into Jed's arms. She closed her eyes and rested her head against the warmth of his chest, listening to his strong and steady heartbeat beneath.

He edged back and kissed her firmly on the mouth. 'Don't

ever leave me again,' he growled as he crushed her to him once more.

'I won't,' she whispered. They stayed like that for a few more moments, both taking their fill of each other. Jed pulled back first and looked down into her face. Tears had welled in her eyes and he tenderly wiped them away.

'I love you, Sally. More than you could ever know,' he said, for only her to hear.

'I know just how much that is because that's how much I love you,' she told him solemnly.

Jed lowered his head and kissed her, once, twice, three times. 'I still can't believe you're really here. This last weekend was—'

'I know,' she cut him off, and held him close once more.

'I'm sorry to intrude,' Beatrice said, and Sally quickly turned to face her mother, Jed's arm still draped heavily on her shoulders.

'Sorry, Mum. This is Jed McElroy. The man I love.'

Beatrice smiled politely as she shook Jed's hand. 'Nice to meet you. I wish it was under different circumstances. Please, tell me the news on my husband.'

'Let's sit down.' They all complied and Jed, with his chair close to Sally's, began. 'His pelvis is fractured but it needs to settle. Alex and I will review it in a few days' time with further radiographs to see if it warrants an operation. Norman's right femur and tibia are fractured, as are his left tibia and the left second and third metatarsals. His right humerus, radius and ulna are fractured and there's a minor fracture of his left elbow. Thankfully, his skull shows no sign of fracture and he regained consciousness about ten minutes before Theatre.

'Alex and Jordanne have finished nailing the right femur, fixed both tibiae and strapped his foot. They were starting on the humerus when you called through so they should be done in about an hour.'

Jed and Sally patiently answered Beatrice's questions. She was desperately trying to anticipate what would need to happen within the next four to six weeks while Norman began to recover.

'Don't worry about things too much, Mum. Chances are he'll be barking out orders again in no time,' Sally told her, and this time when she said it there was no hint of disgust in her tone. What Jane had said that morning had filled Sally with a resolve towards reconciliation. She wouldn't back down, wouldn't bow to his demands. Instead, she wanted to try reaching out to him, agreeing to disagree but still working at forming a relationship between them.

Jed stayed with them until Alex phoned through to say Norman was on his way to Recovery. Beatrice was shown to her husband's side and, apart from a slight sob at the sight of him, she remained calm and strong—just as she was positive her husband would want her to be.

'Let me hold you again,' Jed said to Sally when the tearoom was finally empty. Alex had gone to ICU to make sure everything was ready for Norman's transfer, and Jordanne had decided to spend a few minutes with Joel.

'I missed you,' Sally said after he'd bent his head to kiss her more thoroughly than before.

'The feeling is mutual. I'm glad you went to see my parents.'

'Me, too. I was amazed when my car steered its way over there, but when I thought about it, where else would I feel so comforted than in the house where you grew up? Your parents are remarkable people. Your mother has such wonderful insights. She should have been a counsellor.'

'She's had that said to her often enough before but she knows her gift for helping people see things from a different perspective is one that should only be used on those around her.'

'That's nice.' Sally nodded. 'She told me that even though we were apart, we were still communicating. It made me realise that we weren't using the right words before. Let's always try, Jed, to *really* communicate—to speak the words that need saying and leave out the words that don't.'

He took her face in his hands and kissed both of her cheeks softly and then her lips. 'Sounds like a terrific idea to me.' He continued to gaze at her. 'You look incredible.'

Sally looked down at her attire. 'In Jordanne's old clothes?'

'Yes. Especially in those old clothes. It's a statement that says you're happy with yourself and don't care what anyone else thinks.'

'I *am* happy, Jed. For the first time, I feel as though I'm getting to know myself—and I want you to be there every step of the way on my self-discovery.'

'I thought you'd never ask,' he replied, and kissed her once more. 'Hungry?'

Sally thought for a moment and realised she hadn't eaten since that morning when she'd sat on his parents' verandah. Neither she nor her mother had been able to stomach food on the flight to Canberra. 'Yes, come to think of it.'

'I think the cafeteria has closed. Let's check on your father before heading to the shops. We're bound to find something there.'

Norman was stable but still sleeping off the effects of the anaesthetic. Beatrice declined their invitation to join them, as Sally had thought she would, but they'd wanted to offer all the same.

'Why did you and my father meet this morning?' Sally asked once they were seated in a restaurant that was quite quiet now that the lunchtime rush was well and truly over. The waitress had taken their order and brought over their drinks. Sally stirred some sugar into her hot cup of tea while she waited for Jed's reply.

'I'd gone to the clinic to get some work done and he called my mobile, demanding to see me again. When he arrived, I told him that his objective in using me to get to you wouldn't work. When he asked why not, I told him that I hadn't seen you since Friday evening after you'd found out what had transpired that morning. He didn't seem too pleased.'

'Oh, I'm not surprised,' Sally responded, her body instantly tensing. 'That's because he had no control over you *and* he'd already donated expensive equipment to the Institute.'

'That's what I thought at first.' Jed nodded.

Sally looked at him. 'What do you mean?'

'I can't explain it.' He took Sally's hand in his. 'It was a look in his eyes, one of...I don't know...sadness.' Jed shrugged.

Sally thought about what Jane had said that morning. Perhaps she *had* been jumping to conclusions where her father was concerned. 'You may be right.'

'Really?' Jed asked, surprised at her attitude.

'Yes. Something your mother said this morning. It's made me think.'

'Sounds like my mother,' Jed said with a smile on his face. His mobile phone shrilled to life. 'Excuse me.'

Sally sipped her tea while Jed concluded the quick phone call. She watched him closely. She could tell he was on the phone to the hospital, and when his gaze met hers, she knew she had been mentioned.

'Anything wrong?' she asked cautiously when he'd finished the call.

'No. That was Recovery. Your father is asking to speak to you.'

Sally felt the world stop spinning. 'He wants to speak to me?' she said, and Jed nodded.

'Finish your tea. Let's go.'

As they walked back to the hospital, Jed's arm around Sally, she tried not to think of all the reasons *why* her father would want to talk to her. Every time in the past it had been to tell her she'd done something wrong. What was it now? she wondered.

'You'll find out soon enough,' Jed whispered in her ear as they rode the lift to Recovery.

'Can you read my mind now?' She forced herself to smile up at him.

Jed planted a quick kiss on her lips. 'No, but I *can* read

your body language. You're as tense as can be. Relax, Sally. Remember, I'm here to support you through whatever happens.'

She hugged him close to her. 'That means so much to me, Jed.'

He kissed her again as the lift doors opened. 'To me, too.'

Jed went with Sally into Recovery but stayed at the nurses' station as she crossed to her father's bedside.

Beatrice stood up when she saw Sally and hugged her daughter. She had tears in her eyes and wiped at them with a lace handkerchief. 'I'll see if I can rouse him,' she said softly.

Seconds later, Sally's father opened his eyes.

'Sally.' His voice was raspy and she instantly gave him some ice chips. 'Thank you.'

At his words, Sally nearly fell over. Her father had *never* thanked her for anything in her entire life.

'Something I haven't said often enough,' he said with a small smile, and tried to raise his hand out to her. Sally grasped it as the smile left his face. '"Sorry" is another word you'll have to help me get used to saying.'

She wondered, for a fleeting moment, whether her father had sustained some sort of concussion but the thought was quickly whisked away. This was something different and she'd seen it quite a few times before but had never experienced it.

Her father had just come through a near-death experience and he was actually *allowing* it to change him. It was obvious from the fact that he'd not only *said* the word 'sorry' but was asking for *help* to say it! Tears misted in Sally's eyes and she gave his hand a little squeeze.

'Dad…'

Norman's lower lip began to quiver. 'The last time you called me that, you were about five.'

Sally nodded. 'I remember.'

'Help me, Sally. Help me to become a better person. I watched you do it with your grandfather…' He trailed off.

Tears fell from Sally's lashes as she blinked her eyes and sniffed. 'He forgave you,' Sally said earnestly.

'That means a lot,' Norman answered. 'But what would mean even more is if…you'll forgive me.'

'Oh, Dad,' Sally sobbed, and pressed her lips to his hand. 'You have no idea how long I've waited for this day. I began to think it would never happen.'

'Facing death—it's scary.' The words were barely audible but Sally heard them—she read the terror in his eyes. Norman Bransford had finally come to realise that he was a mortal man and that his life could be over in an instant. 'Your mother has forgiven me…'

'I do, too, Dad.' Sally was so overwhelmed with emotion that she whispered, 'And I love you.'

Norman disengaged his hand from his daughter's and placed it on top of her head. His thumb gently rubbed her hair. 'I love you, too, baby.'

Sally raised her head at his words and when she looked into his eyes she knew he meant it. 'I'm sorry it took years for us to say these words, but I'm so thankful that it's finally happened.' She swiped the tears away from her face and sniffed once more.

'I hope I haven't ruined things between you and Jed. He saved my life, you know.'

Sally glanced over at Jed. 'No. I didn't know.'

'My heart stopped beating when they took me out of the car. Your young man revived me. After what I'd said to him, I…I wouldn't have blamed him if he'd let me die. I was awful to both him and you—insulting both of you—yet still he breathed the breath of life into me. I'm so grateful to him for saving my life—giving me a second chance. A chance to make it up to you and your mother. I won't ruin it.' Norman stopped and closed his eyes.

'Oh, Dad.' Sally slipped her fingers into his hand and squeezed again. 'It's a new beginning for all of us,' she whispered, before sliding her fingers to her father's wrist to check his pulse. 'Are you feeling some pain?' she asked cautiously.

'A little.'

'Why didn't you say so?' she admonished, but not harshly. She indicted to Jed and he walked across to them.

'I wanted to say these things, just in case anything else happens.'

'Everything is going to be fine. You, me and Mum. We're all going to be fine,' she told her father forcefully.

He smiled, his eyes still closed. 'That's my girl.'

'Problem?' Jed asked.

'His pulse is up and he's experiencing some pain,' Sally informed him.

Jed checked Norman's chart. 'I'll take care of it.'

A few minutes later, Norman had received an injection of analgesics and was sleeping peacefully again. Sally made sure her mother was all right and that a bed had been organised for Beatrice for that evening before she and Jed left the hospital.

'What a day,' Jed remarked as they walked to his car. 'We can come back later, if you like, and check on your father.'

Sally shook her head. 'I'll just call. He has Mum and she'll make sure everything is taken care of. I want to give them some time alone—*really* alone—to talk things through.'

Jed only nodded and drove to her town house. He made dinner while she showered and changed. When they were snuggled up on the lounge, their appetites satisfied from the delicious meal Jed had prepared, Sally leaned over and kissed him.

'Thank you,' she said.

'For what?'

'For saving my father's life.' When he didn't say anything she elaborated. 'Performing CPR at the accident site.'

Jed frowned. 'How…? I mean, who told you?'

'My father did.'

'How did he know? He was unconscious.'

Sally shrugged. 'Stranger things have happened. Thanks to you he's had a change of heart and realised that the important things in life are the people around him. I know you'd just say it was part of your job but…you're a wonderful man, Jed McElroy, and I love you.'

Jed pressed his lips to hers and gathered her closer. The scent of his body, the feel of his hair, the touch of his slightly unshaven cheek across hers—all of it made Sally shudder with delight. She'd finally found the place to call home. It was in Jed's arms, in his life, in his heart, with him in hers.

'It's not too bad,' Sally said as Jed pulled his Jaguar into his parents' garage. He gave her a puzzled frown. 'The drive between Canberra and Sydney on a Friday night. Only three hours on a decent road and we're at our parents' houses.'

Since the reconciliation between Sally and her father almost two weeks ago, she had been more than happy for her parents to live *this* close. She climbed out of the car and stretched her legs. 'I'd like to go and see dad tonight after we've had dinner with your family,' she suggested. 'I still can't believe that he took Gordon Partridge apart like that—telling him not to ruin his daughter's life.' Sally shook her head, remembering. 'I was a little concerned that Dad might pop a few stitches, but he kept his cool in his negotiations with Gordon and calmly told him that *he'd* pull his money from the merger if Gordon *didn't* give Alice control over her own life.'

Sally smiled at Jed. 'The changes in Dad are…miraculous. It's been two days since he was transferred to Sydney from Canberra and I'm starting to miss him.' She laughed with amazement at her own feelings, delighting in them.

Jed came around to her side of the car and gathered her into his arms. 'If you want to see your parents, then that's what we'll do, my darling.'

Sally blushed and smiled at him. 'I like it when you call me that. It makes me feel…special.'

'You are.' His gaze was intense with love and he kissed her passionately. Sally wound her arms about his neck, knowing she would *never* get enough of him.

'Let's get the bags later,' he murmured against her ear. 'The family are waiting inside.'

Sally shivered slightly at the breeze. 'So much for it being spring now, it's still cold.'

They went inside the front door and into the darkened lounge room.

'Where is everyone?' Sally asked.

'Perhaps they're all out the back.'

The instant Jed said the words, the lights flickered on and people jumped out from behind furniture shouting, 'Surprise!'

Sally laughed at all of them. 'Why are you surprising us? I thought this was *Joel's* welcome-home party.'

'And he's been welcomed,' Joel said from behind her, and she turned to find him sitting in a wheelchair with a large grin on his face.

'So what's with the surprise?' Sally asked as she glanced around the room. Brothers, sisters, nieces, nephews as well as Jed's parents, they were all there. 'What's that?' She pointed to a camera contraption on the bookshelf, a long cable running from it.

'That's a digital camera,' Jed replied from behind her.

'Why?' Sally turned and looked at him. He had a look of a man completely in control and she instinctively knew he was up to something. 'What's going on, Jed?'

'I think it's time for the cake,' Jane commented, and quickly rushed out of the room, grinning like a Cheshire cat.

'Cake? Is it someone's birthday?' Sally asked as she once more looked around at all the smiling McElroys. She couldn't help laughing at their goofy expressions. 'Come on. Jordanne?' Her friend just smiled and shook her head. 'Will someone, please, tell me what's going on?' She laughed again and was surprised that she didn't feel at all nervous.

'I know you don't like being out of control, Sally,' Jed placated her, 'but this time you'll just have to be patient and wait for your cue.'

'My cue?' She looked up into his eyes and saw mischief dancing there. 'All right,' she acquiesced. 'I'll be patient.' She glared at the camera. 'But just tell me why the camera is there.'

'Because your parents are watching your every action through a computer set up in your father's hospital room.

Wave!' Jed picked up Sally's hand and shook it from side to side in an imitation wave.

'My *parents*?'

'No more questions.' Jed kissed her lovingly. 'Trust me.'

'Ready?' Jane called.

'When you are, Mum,' Jed replied, and smiled at Sally.

Sally watched as Jane brought a large cake into the room and placed it on the coffee-table. On it was piped, CONGRATULATIONS, SALLY AND JED.

Sally wasn't at all sure what to make of it, so she turned to Jed. Her gaze met with thin air and she quickly lowered her gaze to find him down on one knee. Realisation dawned on her face and she clapped both hands over her mouth.

'Sally Elizabeth Bransford.' He held out his hand for one of hers and she peeled her right hand away from her astonished mouth.

'Wrong one,' Jordanne whispered.

Sally quickly changed hands, giving Jed her left one, her gaze transfixed on his.

'Sally,' he began again, and at his words the family faded into the background as she focused solely on the man before her. 'I love you with all my heart. With you, I have discovered a person who is my equal in every way. Intellectually, physically, spiritually—everything. Please, become my wife so that we can share our lives completely, in every aspect there is.'

Sally's heart was pounding loudly in her ears, her breathing was rapid, her knees felt as though they would buckle and the butterflies in her stomach were doing somersaults. She wet her dry lips and smiled down at him.

'Yes,' she whispered. 'How could I possibly refuse the man who is my soul mate? I love you, Jed.'

Jed held onto her hand while he rose to his feet before gathering her into his arms and sealing their public declarations with a mind shattering kiss. Thankfully, when Jed lifted his head he kept his arm securely around her because Sally was still swooning from the moment.

'Congratulations,' John McElroy said from behind his son,

and Jed turned, giving his father his free hand which was heartily shaken. The phone rang and Jane called as she raced to get it, 'That will be your parents.'

Jordanne hugged her friend close. 'Welcome, my new sister.'

The next few hours passed in a haze, but finally Jed and Sally managed to escape into the library to have some time alone. Sally watched as Jed lit the fire, marvelling at the way his jeans pulled around his thighs. He stripped off his jumper and she smiled seductively, admiring his physique.

He turned and interpreted her gaze. 'Patience, Dr Bransford,' he replied, his own look filled with desire. He settled down on the lounge beside her and Sally went willingly into his arms. 'I've made an appointment for us to go shopping tomorrow morning for an engagement ring.'

'You didn't want to choose one for me?' Sally asked, testing him.

'No. I want you to have whichever one you like the best.'

Sally snuggled in, rubbing her face against his chest. 'I love you the best.'

When he didn't say anything she pulled back and looked at him. He simply smiled down at her with love.

'I'd like you to take a breath, Sally, and from now on that phrase will have an entirely different meaning,' he told her as his head slowly made its descent.

'With pleasure,' she told him, and took a *very* deep breath!

MILLS & BOON®

Makes any time special™

Copyright © Harlequin Enterprises Limited 1997
All rights reserved

Mills & Boon publish 29 new titles every month. Select from...

Modern Romance™   Tender Romance™

Sensual Romance™

Medical Romance™   Historical Romance™

MAT2

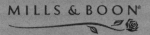

Medical Romance™

EMOTIONAL RESCUE by *Alison Roberts*

Newly qualified ambulance officer Hannah Duncan
soon realises that she loves her job – and her
colleague Adam Lewis! But he doesn't want children,
and Hannah already has a toddler of her own. Will
she be able to help rescue Adam from the demons of
his past and give them all a future?

THE SURGEON'S DILEMMA by *Laura MacDonald*

Catherine Slade knew she was deeply attracted to her
boss, the charismatic senior consultant Paul
Grantham. She also knew he had a secret sorrow
that she could help him with. If only a relationship
between them wasn't so forbidden…

A FULL RECOVERY by *Gill Sanderson*

Book two of Nursing Sisters duo

If he is to persuade emotionally bruised theatre nurse
Jo to love again, neurologist Ben Franklin must give
her tenderness and patience. But when she does
eventually give herself to him, how can he be sure
she's not just on the rebound?

On sale 3rd August 2001

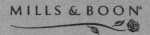

A Perfect Family

An enthralling family saga by bestselling author

PENNY JORDAN

Published 20th July

4 FREE

books and a surprise gift!

We would like to take this opportunity to thank you for reading this Mills & Boon® book by offering you the chance to take FOUR more specially selected titles from the Medical Romance™ series absolutely FREE! We're also making this offer to introduce you to the benefits of the Reader Service™—

- ★ FREE home delivery
- ★ FREE gifts and competitions
- ★ FREE monthly Newsletter
- ★ Exclusive Reader Service discounts
- ★ Books available before they're in the shops

Accepting these FREE books and gift places you under no obligation to buy, you may cancel at any time, even after receiving your free shipment. Simply complete your details below and return the entire page to the address below. *You don't even need a stamp!*

YES! Please send me 4 free Medical Romance books and a surprise gift. I understand that unless you hear from me, I will receive 6 superb new titles every month for just £2.49 each, postage and packing free. I am under no obligation to purchase any books and may cancel my subscription at any time. The free books and gift will be mine to keep in any case.

M1ZEA

Ms/Mrs/Miss/Mr ....Initials.......................................
                                                   BLOCK CAPITALS PLEASE
Surname ....
Address ....

....

....Postcode..............................

Send this whole page to:
UK: FREEPOST CN81, Croydon, CR9 3WZ
EIRE: PO Box 4546, Kilcock, County Kildare (stamp required)